Black Ceremonies

Black Ceremonies
by
Charles Black

Parallel Universe Publications

First Published in the UK in 2015
Collection © Charles Black 2015
Cover © Paul Mudie 2015

The Obsession of Percival Cairstairs © 2004. Originally published in Eldritch Blue: Love and Sex in the Cthulhu Mythos

A Fistful of Vengeance © 2006. Originally published in Hell's Hangmen: Horror in the Old West

Death on the Line © 2006. Originally published in Late Late Show

Tourist Trap © 2006. Originally published in Forgotten Worlds #4

A Bit Tasty © 2007. Originally published in Late Late Show

The Coughing Coffin © 2007. Originally published in Nemonymous 7: Zencore

To Summon a Flesh-Eating Demon © 2007. Originally published in The Black Book of Horror

The Revelations of Dr Maitland © 2007. Originally published in Fiction #3, reprinted in Best New Zombie Tales (2010)

The Necronomicon © 2013. Originally published in Cthulhu Cymraeg

Call of the Damned © 2014. Original to this collection

Face to Face © 2014. Original to this collection

The Madness Out of the Sea © 2014. Original to this collection

The Strombolli Collection © 2014. Original to this collection

ISBN: 978-0-9574535-5-5

Parallel Universe Publications, 130 Union Road, Oswaldtwistle, Accrington, Lancashire, BB5 3DR, UK

CONTENTS

The Obsession of Percival Cairstairs   7

Call of the Damned   21

The Revelations of Dr Maitland   29

Tourist Trap   39

Face to Face   53

The Coughing Coffin   65

The Madness Out of the Sea   73

Death on the Line   91

The Necronomicon   99

A Bit Tasty   107

A Fistful of Vengeance   113

To Summon a Flesh-Eating Demon   127

The Strombolli Collection   153

THE OBSESSION OF PERCIVAL

CAIRSTAIRS

"Farringdon, please wait." The tramp wheezed as he grabbed my arm. I was about to tell the fellow to be off when I realised he had called me by name. I looked a little closer and was stunned to see that I recognised the face that was hidden by a beard and several layers of dirt.

"Good God! Cairstairs, is that you?"

He nodded his head in response.

I hadn't seen Percival Cairstairs for quite some considerable time, and you can be sure that this encounter came as something of a shock. It was hard to believe that the dishevelled, haggard fellow who accosted me in the middle of a busy London street was really him. For Cairstairs was normally a quite elegant fellow. Within society he was considered the model of fashionable standards. We were never particularly close, yet I felt I could not ignore him. I hailed a cab and despite the protests of the driver – who was reluctant to transport what he termed "a down-and-out" – I took Cairstairs home with me.

"Farringdon, I must account for how I come to be like this." He tried to explain his situation.

But I forestalled him. "Wait, old man," I said. "Save your explanation for later. You can tell me everything once I have got you home and you have cleaned yourself up."

As I have already said we were not close friends, but I could not leave a fellow gentleman in his situation and I must admit I was curious to learn how he had fallen to so low a station.

After he had bathed and shaved, and then ravenously devoured a substantial meal, we settled in my study with a particularly fine bottle of brandy.

Cairstairs gave a brief smile and said, "What is it they say, the condemned man ate a hearty meal?"

Puzzled by his remark, I asked, "Whatever do you mean?"

"I must make my confession, Farringdon. Of course I have been a fool. I have meddled with things I do not understand and done things that no sane man would contemplate doing."

Despite the warmth of the log fire, a chill went along my spine at his sinister words. He was now wearing some of my clothes and, whilst not as fashionable as the clothes of his own wardrobe would have been, he looked more like his old self. Yet the Cairstairs who sat in the chair opposite me looked older: he had become gaunt, and his hair was thinner and turning grey.

"Well, old man, what's it all about? How on earth did you come to be in such a position?" I asked.

Cairstairs took another drink from his glass and then proceeded to recount a most incredible and disturbing story.

"It will come as no great revelation that my tale begins with a woman. Audrey Manning. Ah, yes, I see you recall her. A real beauty; it should be no surprise that I fell in love with her the first time I saw her. I tried to woo her, but to my great astonishment she remained indifferent to me." Cairstairs paused for a moment in contemplation, and shook his head.

I had met Miss Manning once. She did have a certain attractiveness, yet there was something about her that I cannot quite put my finger on, that I found unappealing.

Nevertheless, rejection would have come as a shock to Cairstairs. He was the sort of handsome fellow that normally women would throw themselves at.

Cairstairs continued. "It turned out she was in love with a man called Frederic Hyde. How could she prefer that fool over me?"

"Frederic Hyde? I don't think I know him, old man."

"The fellow is a veritable Rasputin. Hairy is the best way to describe him. His dark hair is long and lank, and he has a full beard. In fact, he has hair all over his body; never before have I seen so hirsute a man. How could she bear to touch him or in turn be touched by him?

"I determined that I would become the object of Audrey's affections. At first, I thought of it as a challenge, but no matter what method I tried to seduce her, they all ended in failure. I could not accept this.

"Then I found out that Audrey was interested in the occult. Now you probably know that I had always looked upon that sort of thing as a load of childish nonsense, but if that was what it would take, then I too would become an occultist. Of course, at first my interest was superficial – it was really just a ploy to make myself seem more appealing to Audrey.

"And it worked, at least to an extent. When she learned I had taken an interest in these matters, her attitude towards me thawed and I thought at last I was getting somewhere. It turned out, however, that although she had become friendlier she still preferred Hyde. You see in occult circles – where he is known as Lord Belphagor – Hyde is considered a master wizard and high priest of their strange religion. And what a strange religion. Gods so utterly alien – outré beings inimical to mankind – it is hard to believe that anyone would worship them. Yet they do, and I was to join their ranks. You see, I realised that if I wanted Audrey to be mine, I would have to take this occult business seriously and become more adept at hocus-pocus than Hyde." Cairstairs paused to refill his glass before continuing his tale.

"I studied works of esoteric lore, books by men like Prinn, Roland, and Von Junzt, the grimoires of medieval sorcerers, even some tracts by oriental mystics. Volumes of tediousness and madness that made my head ache. But I persevered with my studies of the black arts, and a gruesome initiation ritual saw me gain membership of the coven. "

Cairstairs held up a hand to silence the question I was about to ask about the nature of the ritual. "I will not say, Henry."

Instead, he said, "The coven met regularly at a place called Stannard's Grave. I don't know if you know it?"

I shook my head. "I cannot say as I do."

"Well, there is no reason that you should. It's a small place in the country, hardly even a village. It's in the middle of nowhere, and it is not the sort of place any respectable fellow should want to be visiting. There are a few houses, a hostelry, and a rundown church no longer used for any sort of Christian service. The locals are a rough lot – no doubt inbreeding is rife. It is the sort of place I imagined Frederic Hyde came from, but I was wrong. Imagine my surprise when I learnt that Audrey was born there. And there is one more grisly thing about Stannard's Grave: in the middle of the village there stands a gallows."

"In this day and age? They don't use it do they?"

Cairstairs did not answer immediately but got up from his chair and paced around the room. It was as if he were having doubts about telling me any more, but eventually he made up his mind and went on.

"Oh yes, Henry, they do."

"Surely not!" I was aghast. "But that's barbaric."

"I know you will find this hard to believe, but the hanging is the least of it."

"You'd better go on." Despite being appalled by this revelation, I was also intrigued, if still a little sceptical.

Cairstairs resumed his seat and his story. "As is traditional there were thirteen of us in the coven. Apart from Lord Belphagor, Audrey, and myself the other ten were five men and five women. You would be shocked if I were to tell you who some of those others were. Suffice it to say that several of them hold positions of power and influence. Sometimes we held our

10

rites in the church, a decayed and ruinous building. The interior trappings have long since vanished. Apart, that is, from the crosses that are now all upside down. At other times around the gallows, always with some unfortunate swinging from the gibbet."

I drained my glass and hastily refilled it. This was turning into a quite disturbing confession.

"Oh, the ceremonies we held. We performed the Black Mass, and strange dark rites that were old before the drowning of Atlantis. We summoned demons and fiends from the blackest pits of hell, made bloody sacrifice to the Old Ones.

"I have taken the Left Hand Path, Henry, and made the pilgrimage to accursed Chorazin. Hocus-pocus I called it, but that was a delusion I did not suffer long. Black magic is a real and powerful force, and although names like Nyarlathotep and Shub-Niggurath will seem like mere mumbo jumbo to you, they are the source of that power. I have ventured through the Gate of Spheres and journeyed to the spaces beyond the stars. Ah, God, Farringdon, if you did but know the cosmic gulfs I have crossed, the inconceivable revelations I have conceived. The veil has truly been lifted from my eyes."

Cairstairs was becoming agitated. "Calm down, Cairstairs," I urged, pouring him some more brandy. "Here, have another drink."

"I made a pact with one of the Old Gods: the Black Man, and signed my name in blood; not just my own. I would serve the Great Old Ones and in return I would gain sorcerous power, and ultimately Audrey would be mine."

Cairstairs paused whilst I added another log to the fire. Even though it was burning well the room seemed to have grown cold.

"At last Audrey realised the error of her ways. You see, I had cast a spell, an enchantment of attraction between us, and this, along with the fact that I was proving to be more adept at

11

sorcery than Lord Belphagor, had turned her affections from Hyde to myself. Or so I thought.

"Eventually I usurped Hyde's position as the head of the coven, and as Audrey's lover, though I do not know whether it was his loss of command or of Audrey which angered him more." Cairstairs allowed himself a humourless laugh before continuing. "He found us one day making love inside a pentagram drawn on the church floor. He was furious and swore revenge. It's laughable to think that this outraged him when our depraved ceremonies made the orgies of Roman emperors seem tame.

"I had wondered how Audrey could stand to be touched by Hyde. In those ceremonies I was to learn she could endure the caress of things much more loathsome. In fact, endure is the wrong word. Oh, how she relished Their touch. I should have been sickened, but it is a sign of how far under her spell I have fallen. It was an experience that I too came to welcome. Yes, it was I, not Audrey who was under a spell for it was she who had the real power. Hyde had been the master of the coven, but he was just a figurehead."

I banished the unwholesome images that came unbidden to mind, and said, "I do not wish to sound like some sort of misogynist, old boy, but women have ever used their charms to get what they want."

"Oh, Audrey knew the influence she had over men: how she could bend them to her will, especially me. She proclaimed herself, 'The daughter of Nyarlathotep. The Bringer of Madness'. I believe she truly believed it and I suppose she was right, for I acknowledge I have lost my sanity. My desire for Audrey has spurred me on into actions so abhorrent I shudder to think of them. I have wallowed in blasphemy, but all of it, Henry, I did for love."

Cairstairs spoke of love, but it seemed more like lust to me. It seemed he had read my mind for he suddenly began to rave.

12

"Do you think me mad, Henry? Love, or lust if you prefer, can make the best of men act irrationally. We are all slaves to our emotions, and love is the most dangerous; that is what They will use, what will be our downfall."

At that moment I did indeed suspect that Cairstairs was mad. I thought he must be for the things that he was telling me were not possible.

"*They* are there waiting beyond, Their malign presence unknown. They seek our destruction, but first they shall make us mad. They are an insidious evil corrupting our passions, manipulating them to bring about our ruin. Mankind is doomed, Henry.

"Audrey was their instrument – I see that now – but it does not matter; even now I still love her."

All this wild talk was most disturbing. I could well believe Cairstairs was involved in some sort of devil worship, but to actually believe in the existence of these devilish gods and their sinister machinations was too much. Surely this coven was a depraved group of drug addicts.

Cairstairs needed help. I began to make a suggestion. "There is someone I know who might be able to help. His name is the Reverend William Henry Shaw and he has had some experience with matters of black magic." Although I felt it was the help of a psychiatrist that he really needed. "Perhaps—"

Cairstairs laughed. "Ha, Christianity! Faith of the feeble. What use is that dying religion?"

"Steady on, old man."

"I'm sorry, Henry. It's too late for Jesus to save me now. I've sold my soul, and believe me it's a soul stained the darkest black." He groaned before continuing. "No, Farringdon, it is too late for that."

"But—" I began to protest.

"No," he interrupted again. Abruptly his mood changed and he began to cry. "Henry, Audrey is dead. Frederic Hyde killed her and now he seeks my blood."

For a moment, Cairstairs sat quietly crying, whilst I contemplated this latest shocking revelation, and then – somewhat appropriately – I was startled by a long wailing cry. As ridiculous as this may seem it sounded like the howl of a wolf. I shuddered as I recalled Cairstairs description of Frederic Hyde.

The wail roused Cairstairs and he began to speak again. "You see, he has even been able to track me here."

Cairstairs got up and crossed to the window; he drew back the curtain a little and stood staring out for a short while, then he closed it and began to pace around the room.

"Audrey may be dead, but we will not be separated for long. Death cannot keep us apart! She rests now in the churchyard at Stannard's Grave, but I will be reunited with her. I have found the means to do it and upon the night of Halloween we will be reunited."

We had finished the brandy, and I excused myself from the room to fetch another bottle. Only to find upon my return that Cairstairs had fallen asleep in his chair. I put a blanket over him and left him sleeping. Then after checking that all the doors and windows were locked, I retired to my bedroom. However, I slept little that night, for I had a madman in my study and perhaps another prowling around my home.

My thoughts raced as I thought of the crazed tale Cairstairs had told. I did not know how much of his bizarre story to believe. I wondered if I should inform the police. At the very least, I felt that Cairstairs should see a doctor, and tomorrow I would arrange an appointment with one.

However, it was not to be, for in the morning I found that Cairstairs had gone.

I never saw Cairstairs again, yet that was not the end of the story. That day I had a visitor; he did not give his name and he was not looking for me but Percival Cairstairs. I have no doubt that he was Frederic Hyde. Even now, I shudder to recall him – oh yes, there was the touch of the wolf to him. I feel sure that if there are such things as lycanthropes then he was the strongest evidence of their existence.

With the passage of time I had dismissed what Cairstairs had said as the ravings of an opium addict.

But I was unaware of the horror that awaited me later that year.

I was on a trip out of London, when quite unexpectedly I happened to see a signpost for Stannard's Grave. Curiosity got the better of me and I visited the ill-omened village.

Stannard's Grave, where I was to witness something so unnatural, so impossible that it leads me to wonder how much else of what Percival Cairstairs had told me was not the product of a feverish imagination but the truth.

The village was just as Cairstairs had described it. Oddly though, the place seemed to be deserted. I tried the public house, the Dancing Man, only to find that it was closed. I took a walk around the churchyard where Cairstairs had said Audrey Manning was buried. This is where I found the villagers. They were gathered around one of the graves, and at first I thought a funeral was taking place. As I drew near however, I saw from the headstone that it was Audrey Manning's grave, and indeed it was open. Cairstairs had never mentioned her having any family alive, and then I recalled his vow that they would be reunited, realising that today was the first day of November, the day after Halloween. For a moment I thought that Cairstairs was dead and was finally being laid to rest with his beloved. Had Frederic Hyde caught up with him?

I stepped closer and saw the coffin at the bottom, but to my horror the coffin had been broken open. I reeled in shock for I knew then that Cairstairs had been reunited with his beloved

15

Audrey Manning.

Ghoulish madness you say; yes, most certainly, but you see the thing is this: the coffin had been broken open from the inside!

Epilogue

Originally, I thought that was where the story of Percival Cairstairs and his obsession ended, but a visit to Henry Farringdon was to set me straight.

"Damn you, Black," Farringdon roared in anger. "I told you that story in the strictest confidence."

He suddenly launched himself at me. His attack took me by surprise, and his hands were at my throat. I suppose Farringdon had every right to be angry with me, nevertheless I had not expected such a ferocious assault.

I was unable to prise his hands from my throat, but fortunately, two white-coated attendants were nearby, and they managed to break his hold, and bind him in a straitjacket.

Farringdon was calmer now, the orderlies had been called away and I considered it perhaps best if I were to leave as well. I wished him goodbye, but he ignored me. Yet, as I reached the door, he spoke. "There is a sequel, you know?"

I turned back, curiosity aroused. "A sequel, Henry?"

"Indeed there is. I'll tell it you, if you like. No doubt, you will fictionalise it for one of your books – but at least I know you will believe me, Black. Anyone else in here will think it just another delusion of my mental state."

He snorted in disgust. "Fools! You and I, Black, we both have had our uncanny experiences." He looked at me conspiratorially. "We know the truth don't we, Black?"

"Yes, Henry," I agreed. And I assure you that I was not merely humouring him. I am not ashamed to admit that I too have had strange encounters with the outré – experiences that had led to my temporary confinement in that self-same hospital that now held Henry Farringdon. That was how we had first met.

Farringdon took a deep breath, then began.

"It was not long after my visit to Stannard's Grave that the dreams began"

"Dreams, Henry?"

"Yes, dreams. Or maybe nightmares."

"Tell me about them," I said.

Henry sighed. "They were dreams of that woman Audrey Manning."

"Go on," I urged.

"Very well," he said, after a moment. "I am ashamed to say they were of a sexual nature."

"You are too hard upon yourself, Henry; there is no shame in that."

"They were of the most depraved nature." Farringdon shuddered.

"Remember I told you that although Audrey Manning was a physically attractive woman, there was always something about her that I found somehow repellent?"

"Yes, I remember."

"Yet despite that, my thoughts were full of her. Day and night, I could think of little else."

Farringdon's face contorted into an expression of anguish. "Ah, Black, I was haunted by a veritable succubus."

Farringdon groaned. "You can be sure I felt revulsion for myself – you see, Black, I wanted her. It was an insane lust, worse than the lust that controlled Percival Cairstairs."

One of the hospital attendants had returned to the cell, or rather this was a different man to those who had restrained Henry. And I noticed now what a particularly hairy individual the man was. Perhaps here was the inspiration for Frederic Hyde. Thankfully, Henry had not noticed his entrance.

"I too was becoming obsessed with her. And I vowed I would find her, and make her mine. You can understand that, can't you, Black?" He looked at me, his eyes full of pleading.

I nodded, and he continued.

"Their trail led me to strange places, and I witnessed strange things." Farringdon shuddered again. "And God help me, I played my part in some of those strange things, too."

"What things, Henry?" I asked.

But he shook his head, and would not tell me.

He remained silent, and for a moment I was worried he would reveal no more.

Thankfully, he took up his story again.

"Yet they always seemed one step ahead of me. But I was tenacious; I would not give up my search."

Farringdon suddenly laughed. "I found them eventually, though."

"Where was that, Henry?" I asked.

He ignored my question; his smile was grim. "Do you remember how Cairstairs had said Frederic Hyde had discovered the pair of them making love?"

I nodded.

"I too found the pair of them together. Entwined. I cannot bring myself to call it making love."

Farringdon's smile disappeared. "Any lingering doubts I had had about what Cairstairs had told me, and what I had seen in Stannard's Grave were banished then."

"You mean—" I began.

"Yes, Black, it was all true. Audrey Manning had been dead,

and somehow Percival Cairstairs had raised her from the grave."

"But surely?"

"God, help me!" Farringdon began to wail. "It should be Percival Cairstairs who is imprisoned in this sanatorium, rather than I. Surely it is he who is insane!"

"Calm down, Henry," I urged. The hirsute attendant was approaching, but I signalled he should keep back.

"You see, Black, Cairstairs had brought Audrey Manning back to life, but it was not a natural restoration to the ranks of the living."

"What are you saying, Henry?"

"Whilst she may have been living and breathing, Cairstairs had been unable to restore her ..." Farringdon seemed at a loss for words.

He began to rock backwards and forwards, moaning, "The decay! The decay!"

The orderly started forward again, and I knew I would have to leave.

"What, Henry?" I gasped; half expecting what Farringdon was about to say, yet needing to hear it anyway.

"Don't you see, Black?" Farringdon suddenly grabbed me by the lapels of my jacket. "Cairstairs was having sex with a living corpse!"

CALL OF THE DAMNED

Like most writers, I am sometimes asked about my influences, and where I get my ideas from. Occasionally people want to know why so many of my protagonists share such similar fates – i.e. horrible deaths or insanity.

I suppose it originates with something that happened one evening, several years ago. I was already penning weird tales at the time but the events that took place that night, and what subsequently transpired were to have a profound influence upon my writing. Circumstances now permit me to reveal what occurred upon that fateful night.

My brother had called round to see me the night it happened. In his usual manner he had just asked what I was working on. "Come up with any more of your horrific tales then?"

"Well, I've got a couple of new titles – 'The Horror in the Hole' and 'The Man Who Collected Skin Diseases' – but no actual stories to go with them so far," I had replied.

He laughed. "Oh, I'm sure you'll come up with something suitably terrible." You will realise that my brother does not hold a high opinion of my writing.

It was at that moment that the telephone rang.

I answered it, and recognised the voice that said, "Ah, there you are. What took you so long?" It was an old friend of mine.

"Hello Julian. How are you?"

"Splendid, old boy. But never mind all that, I've got some important news for you."

"Just a moment, Julian," I stalled him. "It's Julian Cavendish," I informed my brother.

"In that case I'll be off then," he said. "You two will be talking black magic all night. Don't worry, I'll see myself out."

"Okay, carry on, Julian; you've now got my undivided attention," I said, after waving goodbye to my brother.

"Hope I haven't interrupted anything important."

"No, of course not, just my brother making jokes at my expense."

"How is the old scoundrel?"

"Oh, he's his usual self. Listen, I've been trying to contact you. Where have you been?"

"Why, in search of the secret tradition, of course."

Julian Cavendish shared my interest in the occult, but whereas my interest was as research for my stories; Julian was writing an exposé of the black arts.

"You'll remember I have been trying to track down a summoning spell to call the demon, Vorosh."

"Yes, I remember. I thought the spell might be contained in a complete edition of Roland's *Esoteric Revelations*."

A publisher by the name of Visionary Press had produced an extremely limited number of a heavily expurgated edition of *The Grimoire of Esoteric Revelations*. Julian and I were both fortunate to own copies of this obscure work.

Written by the Victorian occultist Charles Roland, and described as: 'the ravings of a madman', the Visionary Press edition barely hinted at the revelations supposedly contained in the complete text. Roland claimed to have had dealings with 'all manner of demons and their kindred', which was why I considered it a likely source for the Vorosh spell.

"That's why I decided to contact the publishers. I thought it was possible that they might possess a complete version from which they had produced their edited edition."

"Any luck?" I asked.

"Huh," he grunted. "I couldn't even get a phone number, and there was no response to the letter I sent them. So, I decided to visit the premises of Visionary Press in person. Imagine my disappointment when I found Helmount House, an abandoned and decaying ruin. Visionary Press had long gone."

"A dead end then?"

"Well, yes. But not to be put off, I managed to track down an address for Ronald Kane."

"Bloody hell, Julian! Kane's not a man to be meddled with."

Although the name of Ronald Kane means nothing to most people – somehow he has avoided coming to the general public's attention – to those involved with the occult however, Kane had become notorious as a practitioner of the black arts.

He was involved in the editing of *Esoteric Revelations*. Some occultists claim that in fact he even wrote it himself, or at least much of that which Visionary Press published.

There were also rumours that Kane believed himself to be the reincarnation of Charles Roland.

"The seekers of recondite wisdom often have to venture along dangerous paths; you should know that, my friend," Julian said. "Anyway, I found out that Kane lives in a village called Barrow Ashton."

"Really? I know it, but I had no idea Kane lived there."

"Oh yes, in a great big Gothic mansion. But Kane refused to see me."

"I must admit I'm not surprised. From what I know of the man, turning up unannounced and uninvited at his residence would not go down well."

"I could not even get an appointment to consult him at a future date. Well, despite yet another setback, I would not be thwarted in my quest. I would take whatever means were necessary to gain access to this rare work, even if it meant breaking the law."

"What are you saying, Julian?"

"Last night I broke into Kane's mansion."

"You did what?" I was astounded by my friend's confession.

"It was, I admit, a most exhilarating experience."

"You are having me on aren't you? I know it's the first of the month but you're a month out for April Fool's Day."

"Of course not, I'm quite serious."

"Hang on. Last night was April the thirtieth – Walpurgis

Night."

"Exactly, I had watched Kane leave earlier that evening – as I had known he would – to attend a Walpurgis Night sabbat."

"My God, you are serious. Have you taken leave of your senses?"

Julian laughed. "I believe I may have, but it was worth it. The contents of Kane's library are staggering – you would have loved it. I thought I had an outstanding collection, but it pales into insignificance compared to Kane's. It ranges from the mundane to the legendary. Never before have I seen such a collection of rare and obscure occult books."

"You don't mean to say he had the *Necronomicon*?"

"Well, he had several, but alas none were the genuine article. I must admit though, that it wouldn't surprise me at all if he had one hidden away there somewhere.

"However, it was *The Grimoire of Esoteric Revelations* that was the object of my quest, and as I suspected Kane's library contained the said volume. And it was obviously a complete text.

"I was tempted to take more than just the *Grimoire* but it was too great a risk and I managed to restrain myself. However, I felt that perhaps the absence of just one book might be overlooked, at least until I had managed to make a copy and anonymously return the original.

"Of course, I could not resist the opportunity of studying some of Kane's ancient and legendary tomes. And I became so engrossed in examining Kane's library that I quite lost track of time.

"I was roused from my studies by a noise. The strange thing is I am unable to find the words to describe how it actually sounded. All I can say – and I know this doesn't make sense – is that it sounded evil, utterly evil, and it made me afraid. God! I have never been so afraid in my life. I had to get out of that house, and yet it could only have been Kane.

"It had to be Kane. The alternative is too disturbing to contemplate, for it is well known that Kane has dealings with things not of the sane world. I told myself that Kane had returned unexpectedly early, and I quickly took my leave."

Julian was right about Kane; several stories circulated among occult circles about the pacts he had made with inhuman powers. There were also whispers of mysterious deaths amongst his rivals.

"Surely, if Kane realises that his copy is missing, the first person he will suspect will be the stranger who had come seeking a meeting with him. You've taken a hell of a risk, Julian."

"It was a risk I was prepared to take. Roland's book is much more disturbing than the admittedly disquieting expurgated edition. My God! The things he writes of, surely he must have passed beyond the veil. You must see it, my friend. You must come round tomorrow."

"Of course I shall. How could I not?" Even I could not resist the lure of a complete *Grimoire of Esoteric Revelations*.

"And you were right, my friend; the incantation to call Vorosh is among its pages. Although I'm sure you can imagine my disappointment when I performed the spell and it did not work."

"What? Julian, I do not know which was the more foolish – stealing from Ronald Kane or attempting to summon Vorosh. I shall have to write a story warning of the dangers of meddling with black magic – a cautionary tale. Why on earth would you want to summon a demon anyway?"

"Nonsense. I haven't stolen from Kane. Just borrowed."

I interrupted. "I doubt he'll see it that way."

"And anyway, as I said, the spell didn't work. Although I'm unsure whether the spell was at fault, or if I got something wrong in the casting."

"You probably had a lucky escape." I noticed that he had not answered my question, but I let it pass.

"Not at all. We shall try the spell tomorrow when you come round. Hello? What's that? That's strange."

"Julian, is everything all right?"

"Yes, of course, my dear fellow. It's just that I can hear something a bit odd."

"Julian, what is it?"

"It's that sound. That evil sound that I heard last night at Kane's house."

"Are you sure? I can't hear anything."

"Of course I'm sure. It's in my house. I can hear it getting louder, coming closer. But I'm being fanciful. There is no way Kane could know that it was I in his library last night. Is there?"

"To be honest, Julian, I wouldn't put anything beyond Kane."

"Look, hang on just a minute, old boy, I'm going to put the phone down a moment to go and investigate. Don't go anywhere, I shan't be a tick."

"Julian, be careful. Remember Kane's reputation. I think it might be a good idea if you got out of there."

"Good God! I'll not run again, last night was one thing, but I'll not be driven out of my own home. I won't!"

"Julian?" But he wasn't listening to me, and I heard the clunk of the phone being put down on his desk.

I continued to listen though, and I heard my friend's footsteps, the opening of his library door. And then I too could hear that strange sound that tormented Julian. I should be able to describe it, its pitch or tone, after all I fancy myself a writer, don't I? And yet I cannot. I cannot even think of anything that it sounded remotely similar to. Julian had described it as evil. And it needs no more description than that, for that is what it was – evil!

Suddenly I heard my friend's shocked cry, "Begone, spawn of the pit!"

Perhaps there was something I could have done to have

helped him. But I remained, as if bewitched, on the end of the telephone. Listening to his panicked recitation of what sounded like a banishing spell. A spell that obviously did not work, for I heard Julian begin to say the Lord's Prayer. A last desperate appeal, the words getting louder and louder. Until finally he must have been screaming them at the top of his voice.

And then suddenly silence.

When I got to Julian's house, I did not bother ringing the doorbell but instead forced the front door open. The hallway was in darkness, and I tried the light switch – but it did not work.

I took a few steps forward, calling Julian's name, but there was no response. The only sound: the crunch of glass under my feet – the light bulb had shattered.

Feeling my way, I went in further – half expecting something to attack me – instead I almost stumbled over something. I crouched down to feel what – although I suppose I already knew that it was my friend. But was he still alive?

Julian always kept a lighter in his pocket, and I managed to find it. Its flickering flame revealed that there was no way that my friend could still live. There were fragments of his skull and brain splattered everywhere. It appeared as if Julian Cavendish's head had exploded.

Of *The Grimoire of Esoteric Revelations*, there was no sign.

Unbelievably, the coroner's inquest deemed Julian's death as death by natural causes.

Because I was a writer of horror fiction, my testimony was dismissed as 'the ramblings of a mind, already prone to macabre thoughts, which had been further disturbed by the death of a friend'. And for my own good, it was decided, that I should spend some time in a mental asylum, to recover from my shock.

I try not to be bitter about this, and instead look upon that period of my life as a positive experience. After all, I suppose I did garner quite a bit of material during my stay, which inspired several of my strange stories.

I recently acquired my own copy of the complete version of Charles Roland's book, and I learned more about the demon called Vorosh. Including a description that described Vorosh: 'Sometimes the demon takes a non-corporeal form that cannot be seen, but only heard. Only the result of its actions can be seen.'

I also found a warning: 'That at the time of the Great Sabbat merely to say the words of the summoning spell is enough to call forth Vorosh.'

Perhaps Julian had inadvertently mouthed the words of the spell whilst at Kane's house, that Walpurgis Night, and brought forth the demon himself – even before he had tried to perform the ritual at his own home.

Or perhaps Ronald Kane had already made a pact with the demon.

Although no trace of his body has been found, Ronald Kane disappeared in mysterious circumstances and is presumed dead.

Perhaps, now that I have repeated my testimony, and if Kane is not really dead, I shall hear that evil sound again.

I will be listening.

THE REVELATIONS OF DR MAITLAND

"Okay, so you don't believe in ghosts?" Dr Andrew Maitland stood at the window, looking out at the moonlit grounds of Endor House.

His host, the businessman Roger Hilton, sat in a comfortable leather armchair. "Correct."

"Well, what do you think happens after we die?" Maitland drew the burgundy-coloured velvet curtains closed.

"We get put in a box in the ground, and rot. Or our bodies get cremated."

"Hmm." Dr Maitland turned his attention to one of the paintings that adorned the study walls. He shuddered. And yet, "Remarkable," was his verdict.

"What's that?"

"This painting." Dr Maitland indicated the picture in question.

Hilton rose from his seat, and joined his friend in examination of the painting. "Dear God!"

The painting was a night-time scene of four figures in a cemetery. At a glance, it appeared they were grave robbers, but closer inspection revealed that these charnel defilers were something less than human, bestial, and disturbingly obscene. By the light of a gibbous moon, the hideous creatures engaged in acts far fouler than the theft of a corpse.

Maitland was impressed. "It's a remarkable piece of work, and a remarkable likeness."

Hilton grunted. "Damned grotesque, if you ask me. Do you think it's worth anything?" Hilton had recently inherited the house and its contents, and this was his first visit to the property. Much of what he had found, he had found not to his taste.

"I don't know." Maitland looked closer. "I can't quite make it out but I think it's signed. Could be Pickman?"

Hilton shrugged. "Doesn't mean anything to me. You like it?"

"No, I don't. I find it terrifying," Maitland paused, "and yet, I also find a certain comfort in it."

"What are those creatures supposed to be anyway? You have some idea, Andrew?"

"Ghouls, I should think."

"Ghouls? Since when did you become an expert about *the children of the night*?" said Hilton doing his best to mimic Bela Lugosi.

Despite his serious mood, Maitland had to laugh.

"Come on, Andrew. My impression wasn't that bad, was it?"

"Roger, the children of the night are wolves."

"Ah, well, ghosts and ghouls. Vampires and werewolves." Hilton snorted in disgust. "Load of rubbish if you ask me."

"You think so?"

"Of course I do!" The businessman sat down again. "The undead. Is that what this is all about?"

Maitland remained contemplating the painting. "Hmm?"

"You asked me, what I thought happened after we die."

"It was the fate of the soul, I had in mind."

"Oh, you mean Heaven and Hell."

"There are other possibilities," Maitland said.

"Heaven or Hell?" mused Hilton. "That's a big question," he said, lighting a cigarette. "Build up the fire, would you, Andrew?"

Dr Maitland added some coal to the flames, then sat in the other armchair.

Apart from the ticking of the clock, and the roar of the fire, the two men sat in silence. Hilton smoking, considering the question, whilst his friend gazed deep into the heart of the fire's flames.

Eventually Hilton delivered his verdict, "Nope. Don't believe in either."

"How about reincarnation?"

Hilton frowned. "What? The belief that we have lived previous lives?"

"Yes, that's it. The rebirth of the soul. The cyclical return of a soul to live another life in a new body."

"No! I most certainly do not." Hilton threw the remains of his cigarette into the fire. "Reincarnation, ghosts and ghoulies, all rubbish. I can't believe we are having this conversation, Andrew. Either we've had too much to drink, or not enough." The businessman reached for the decanter. "How about another?"

"Um, yes, please." Maitland held out his glass for a refill.

"So, where's all this leading?" Hilton topped up their glasses.

"I've been doing some research—" Maitland began, Hilton interrupted with a groan.

"Oh, for goodness sake, Andrew, don't tell me you've been dabbling with some sort of spiritualism."

"No, not spiritualism as such."

"A world of charlatans and fools. I don't know which I despise the more."

Maitland's smile was brief. "Ah, like you, there was a time when I too, would scoff at such things. But that was before—"

Hilton butted in again, "Oh, come on, Andrew. It's nonsense. It must be. I mean, haven't you noticed that everyone who believes in reincarnation has always been someone famous from history? How many of them were Cleopatra or a Roman emperor? Without exception, they have all had previous lives that were glamorous or important. They have been kings and queens, at the very least a Red Indian princess."

Maitland smiled again. "You're exaggerating, Roger. But as I said, I was sceptical myself. Then a colleague told me about a patient of his who claimed to have lived previous lives."

"I don't suppose this was a mental patient was it, old boy?"

Maitland sighed. "Yes, as a matter of fact it was."

"There you are then." Hilton grinned.

"I would have put it down to a delusion myself but the patient was so convincing, and quite lucid – well most of the time – a scientist, who specialised in recondite matters." Maitland shrugged. "I was curious and looked into the matter a bit further."

"A lot further by the sound of it."

"I read some strange books."

"Undoubtedly written by a bunch of cranks."

"Then I began to experiment with a drug called Liao."

"Liao? I've never heard of it. And I'm surprised that you have. I never had you down as someone who would be seduced by this New Age counter culture. You've not been seeing someone behind Barbara's back have you? Having an affair with some young hippie girl?"

"No, of course not. Barbara and I are very happy together."

Hilton hastily apologised. "Of course you are. Sorry, Andrew."

Hilton poured fresh drinks. "Well, tell me about this Liao stuff," he said.

"It's an Oriental concoction known to occultists and alchemists."

"Ah, the mystic East." Hilton smirked. "So, what's it do?"

"It enables the user to travel in time—"

"Travel in time?" roared Hilton, interrupting.

"Not physically of course." Dr Maitland sighed. "It's rather difficult to explain the effect."

"Try."

"Well, I suppose the best analogy would be that it's a form of astral projection." Maitland held up a hand to forestall the comment his friend was about to make. "Roger, the how is not really the important thing. What is important is that it works, and I have found that I had lived many other lives."

Hilton was about to say something about Indian princesses, but Maitland's serious expression changed his mind. He decided it was best to humour his friend.

"All right, suppose I said: prove it to me. Did you bring any of this Liao down here with you?"

"No." Maitland shook his head. "You'd take it if I had?"

"Maybe. Maybe not." Hilton lit up another cigarette. "You did, and came through it unharmed, didn't you?"

"Maybe. Maybe not," Maitland echoed Hilton's own words.

Hilton frowned. "Okay, so how are you going to convince me?" He cut his question short, the rest of it – the words: you haven't gone mad – remained unspoken.

"I'm going to tell you about an occurrence that happened when I was not Dr Andrew Maitland but George Prendergast, a soldier …"

Before putting it back in his jacket pocket, Private George Prendergast kissed the picture of his sweetheart Sally-Ann. Would he ever see her again? he wondered.

He took out his cigarette case, and lit a woodbine, then returned the case to the same pocket as the photograph – over his heart. Prendergast had never smoked before the war. But he had taken up the habit after hearing how Tommy Morsan had escaped death, when a bullet meant for his heart, had struck the cigarette case that he carried.

Around him, his fellow soldiers were going through similar rituals, checking weapons and equipment, and saying prayers. The bombardment of enemy lines had been going on for some time. It would not be long before the signal would come and they would attack.

The signal eventually came, too soon for some, not soon enough for others, and over the top, they went. Charging the enemy. Charging Death himself.

A charge across a patch of muddy, rutted ground. Ground pocked with great craters, shell holes filled with scummy water.

A desolate waste ground where nothing now grew, except the number of corpses. A quagmire of death.

A charge into tangles of barbed wire, and machine guns spitting bullets. Except it could not really be called a charge, the weight of the equipment the men carried, and the treacherousness of the mud, meant that they moved little faster than a walking pace.

Into No-Man's-Land, the zone of death. Soldiers scythed down by the hail of enemy bullets. Shells exploding, hurling men hither and thither. Prendergast was unsure whether the shells were theirs, or those of the enemy. It no longer mattered to the dead men.

"Please God, don't let me die for nothing," Prendergast prayed, certain that his death was certain.

Prendergast repeated the mantra as he progressed towards the enemy.

An orange cloud was drifting towards the advancing troops. "Gas!" Prendergast shouted, struggling to put on his gas mask. Before he had, the force of a nearby explosion threw him to the ground. He remained unmoving, and the battle raged on.

In the distance the guns rumbled, explosions flashed, lighting the grey sky. But that was far off, the battle had moved on.

Private Prendergast realised he was still alive. He wiped his face with his sleeve, did not notice the blood. Instead, he looked around him, and was sick, adding the meagre contents of his stomach to the detritus of human waste that surrounded him. Bodies, and parts of bodies lay everywhere.

He recognised the mangled remains of friends and comrades. There was Private Bobby Owens, or at least his upper half, the rest of the young soldier had been blown to kingdom come. Prendergast giggled, at least the lad would not be complaining about trench foot anymore. Others were beyond recognition.

He heard a groan – someone else was alive. Friend or foe? he wondered. Unsteady on his feet, Prendergast rose.

"What the bleedin' hell …?" he muttered.

He could have sworn he saw a severed arm move, its grasping hand pulling it along.

He shook his head, rubbed his eyes, and laughed nervously.

The arm moved again, the hand clawing the mud, dragging the limb behind it.

Prendergast licked his parched lips. His Enfield rifle was near at hand, he wondered whether that was what the limb was aiming to reach. Prendergast crouched down and grabbed his weapon. He pounced, bayoneting the arm. The hand jerked, clawing, convulsing spasmodically, then was still.

There was more groaning now. Prendergast pulled the blade free, and backed away, almost falling over another body. The soldier moaned. Prendergast recognised a comrade – Dennis Trotter.

"Thank God, you're alive!"

Trotter groaned; his hand reached for Prendergast.

Prendergast bent over the wounded man, shrugging off his army pack. He would not be able to carry that and Trotter back to their own lines.

"Are you hurt badly?" he asked.

Trotter's blood-soaked jacket answered that question. Prendergast opened the jacket, reeled back, retching again. There was no way Trotter could still be alive with that gaping stomach wound.

Yet Trotter raised a hand, grasped Prendergast by the throat, began to squeeze and pull the private down towards him.

Shock kept Prendergast frozen momentarily, and then realisation that a dead friend was choking the life out of him spurred the private into action. He struggled free, and smashed the butt of his rifle into Trotter's face.

Around him men of both sides – including Trotter – were

slowly rising. Men with terrible wounds. Dead men. Private Prendergast began to back away.

They were closing in on him. Staggering and shambling, men that no longer breathed yet groaned and moaned. Some missing limbs, others with gaping wounds spilling entrails.

Staring with sightless eyes. Ruined faces; one corpse entirely headless.

Prendergast watched dazed and amazed. "This can't be happening," he muttered. Hands reached out for him but not all of them.

A Hun, with his guts hanging out, grabbed and pulled free some of his intestines. His intent to use them as a garrotte.

Prendergast fired, his bullet hitting one of the living corpses in the eye. Prendergast was amazed for two reasons. Normally, he would not have achieved such accuracy even if he had tried to aim for the eye. Secondly, the shot had little effect – the walking dead man staggered at the impact, paused a moment, then continued its shambling advance.

Prendergast began to lay about him then.

"I'll be damned if I let a bunch of dead men kill me!" he shouted, stabbing and thrusting his bayonet wildly.

Though bullets had little effect, the blade proved more effective.

Prendergast fought as if possessed by the spirit of a Viking berserker.

Thankfully, whatever perversion of nature that had caused these dead men to rise had only affected this small corner of the battlefield. And hacking and slashing, Prendergast was able to fight his way free.

The zombies continued to pursue him, yet they moved slowly and despite his wounds, and the treacherous conditions of the battlefield, the private was able to outdistance them. Ahead were his own trenches. He would be safe there, he told himself. Realising this he began to laugh.

But Prendergast had become disorientated in the fog of war. And he did not find his way back to the safety of his own lines.

He saw a group of men scouring the battlefield. Perhaps they were searching for wounded, Prendergast thought. They looked up at his approach.

"God almighty!" Prendergast gasped.

There was something wrong with them.

They stood hunched, lean, and grey. Whilst some wore blood-drenched uniforms, others were dressed in tattered rags, the remnants of charnel shrouds. Skin discoloured, faces misshapen, snout-like. Creatures of nightmare, they did not carry rifles in their hands, the talons of these scavengers held gobbets of bloody flesh.

They grinned, exposing stained, canine teeth. Private Prendergast began to scream. And then the ghouls pounced.

"... And my last memory is of the charnel stench of the foul creatures, the agonising pain as their fangs bit into me, and their claws tore the flesh from my still-living body. My body rent apart, and the internal organs ripped free. Thankfully oblivion eventually overcame me, and I found myself Andrew Maitland once again, back in London, in the here and now of nineteen seventy-two," Maitland concluded.

"Good God! I've heard of the horrors of World War One but zombies and ghouls!" Hilton brought his fist down on the arm of his chair. "This Liao, it sounds like it took you on a particularly wild trip. Had you been watching too many damned horror films?"

Dr Maitland ignored the question. "I can understand your scepticism, Roger, and I might too accept your verdict of drug-induced fantasy. But tell me how would you explain this?" Maitland rose from his chair.

"Explain what?"

Maitland took off his jacket. He had lately taken to wearing black polo neck shirts; and he pulled off the one he now wore – to reveal a body covered with an innumerable number of horrific scars.

Hilton gasped, a shocked expression upon his face. "Good God! Andrew, I don't know what to say. How on earth is it possible?"

"That I cannot explain. They are not self-inflicted. The bite marks do not match my dental records, and indeed how on earth would I have been able to bite myself so, even under the influence of such a potent drug?"

Hilton was leaning forward, so as to examine the scars in more detail. "It's not possible. You were definitely alone when you took it?"

Maitland nodded. "Yes. Absolutely. No young hippie girl!"

"Incredible, incredible," Hilton muttered, shaking his head.

Maitland pulled his polo neck back on and returned to his seat. "There's one more thing I feel I should share with you."

"More?"

"Yes, my friend, there's one fact I omitted to tell you."

"Oh?"

"Forgive me, I did not tell you that the user of the Liao, can not only project himself back into the past but also forward into the future. You see, the unfortunate Private Prendergast was a soldier in World War Four!"

TOURIST TRAP

The village sign proclaimed Hexhill as the winner of a Best-Kept Village competition. The American tourist had to agree that it was certainly a well-deserved honour.

At its heart was the village green, complete with pond. Black and white timber-framed houses, and whitewashed cottages, with well-tended gardens, bordered the road that encircled the green.

It was just how he had imagined it.

"The quintessential English village," he said to himself, taking another photograph – this time of the ducks on the village pond. "Pretty as a picture."

The clock on the church tower struck the hour – eleven o'clock, and the tourist decided that St Michael's was where he would begin his tour of the village.

And after St Michael's, he grinned – the Mockingbird, where he would have a pub lunch. Perhaps a roast steak, and a couple of pints of cool beer, which would be most welcome on such a warm August day.

"Good morning!" A cheerful voice hailed him. The tourist closed the lych-gate, and looked round. The greeting was unexpected, because he had not seen anyone in the churchyard.

"Oh, I'm sorry I startled you." A young man rose from where he was kneeling. He had been obscured by a gravestone. He introduced himself, "I'm Reverend Dobson."

The vicar's youthfulness surprised the American – he guessed Dobson to be in his early-thirties – and he had anticipated that the village would have an older man as its incumbent priest.

The tourist raised his hand in greeting, "Good morning, Reverend. I didn't see you there."

"I was just removing these," the vicar explained, holding up a bunch of wilting flowers. "These chrysanthemums are well past their best, I'm afraid. I hope I didn't frighten you Mister ... er ..."

"No, not at all." Although in truth, the sudden greeting had made him jump. "Forgive me. I ought to introduce myself, the name's Joe Buchowski, from the US of A." The American laughed. "Although I guess you probably figured that out, hey?"

The vicar's smile became a sheepish grin. "Well, yes, I must admit I did have my suspicions."

"Don't tell me; it was the shirt, wasn't it?" The tourist wore a particularly garish Hawaiian shirt – predominantly orange and lime green in colour – and blue shorts. He was a large man, in his mid-fifties, whose muscles were running to fat.

In fact, Buchowski was the living embodiment of the vicar's stereotyped image of an American tourist.

But before the vicar could answer, Buchowski went on, "Only an American would have the style and panache to wear a shirt like this."

Unsure whether the American was joking or being serious, the vicar played it safe, and smiled again. "Pleased to meet you, Mr Buchowski."

"Likewise, Reverend," Buchowski responded, shaking the vicar's hand.

"You're here on holiday?"

"Sure am. Say, this is a mighty-fine little village you've got here, Reverend."

The vicar nodded. "Most certainly, we're all very fond of it. And you're sure to get a warm welcome from the villagers, Mr Buchowski."

"Well, it certainly is different from New York. Hey, you mind if I take a look around your church?"

"No, of course not. Please feel free. And if you have any

questions afterwards, I'd be pleased to answer them. You'll find me in the vestry."

After studying the gravestones and monuments in the churchyard, Buchowski entered the church. He knelt and said a prayer for his late wife, Mary; then had a look round.

When his inspection of the stained glass windows, memorial plaques, and effigies of long-dead important locals, was complete, he sought out the vicar.

"Say, Reverend, there ought to be some relatives of mine buried in the graveyard, but I can't seem to find me any. It occurred to me, that perhaps they're buried in the crypt?"

"Relatives?" the vicar queried.

"Yeah, on my mother's side of the family. Left England way back when."

"Ah, that explains it. I should have guessed. As pretty as our village is, it's a bit off the beaten track to be a tourist attraction. Now what was the name?"

"Oh, sorry, didn't I say? Trenair."

The vicar took off his glasses, and polished them absentmindedly. "Trenair?"

"Yeah, that's right. Say, anything the matter, Reverend? You seem to have gone a little pale."

"No, no. I'm quite all right."

"Good. So how come there are no members of the Trenair family buried in the Hexhill graveyard? I have got the right Hexhill haven't I?"

"Oh, yes, you've got the right place. The Trenair's lived in Hexhill, all right."

"So what's the story, Reverend?"

"Look, if you could excuse me a moment there's something I must attend to. But I would be able to join you shortly, and then I could explain why there are no members of the Trenair family

41

buried in our graveyard."

"Well, okay. How about we meet in the local hostelry, I sure could do with a beer."

"Yes, that sounds splendid; Fred Benton serves an excellent pint. I'll see you there. In about a quarter of an hour?"

"Sure thing, Reverend. In fact, I think I'll head there right now."

Reverend Dobson watched Buchowski cross the village square in the direction of the pub, then he hurried off to attend to his urgent business.

Reverend Dobson arrived at the pub accompanied by a pair of burly farmers. Buchowski was sitting at a table, in conversation with some particularly garrulous locals, and enjoying a cigarette and his second pint.

He was having a thoroughly pleasant time: the locals were friendly, the beer was surprisingly good, and he'd liked what he'd seen of the village and the surrounding countryside. It was wonderfully peaceful; and there would be little, if any crime here. I could get used to this, he thought. Hexhill would be a great place to live.

Buchowski had been on the verge of asking his companions about the Trenairs when he spotted the vicar. He stood up and waved. "Hey, Reverend Dobson! Over here. Come and join us."

The vicar paused a moment, saying something to the pair of farmers.

"Let me get you a drink. What'll you have, Reverend?" Buchowski called to the barmaid, "Hey, miss. Another pint for me, and whatever the Reverend is having."

Reverend Dobson shook his head. "No, that's all right, Mr Buchowski, I'll get these."

"Well, if you're sure, then that sure is friendly of you." The tourist sat down again and stubbed out his cigarette.

Reverend Dobson crossed to the bar and spoke to the landlord. Then whilst Benton prepared their drinks, he announced to the locals, "Our American visitor, Mr Buchowski is a descendent of our village." He allowed the murmurs to quieten before continuing. "He is a descendent of the Trenair family."

Buchowski had risen, perhaps expecting a round of applause. He certainly didn't expect the silence and stony looks that he received. Puzzled and embarrassed, he sat down again. The men whom he had been talking with, got up and moved away.

"Hey, Reverend, why the unfriendly reaction? Is there something I should know?" Buchowski asked, as Reverend Dobson joined him.

"Here." The vicar handed him a fresh pint. "Drink some of this."

Buchowski drank, then looked at the vicar for an explanation.

"The Trenairs were notorious in these parts."

Buchowski frowned. "Notorious? In what way?"

"They were witches."

"Witches? No kidding!" Buchowski laughed. "You're having me on, right?"

Reverend Dobson's expression was severe.

"You're not serious?"

"Oh, but I am. Deadly serious."

The American was eager to learn more about his notorious ancestors. "Well, what did they do?"

"Perhaps better to ask: what didn't they do? They were known to consort with the devil. And their evil spells and curses were the bane of many. The villagers, and all for miles around lived in fear of the Trenairs."

Dobson paused to drink, smiled and then continued. "That was until the witch-finder came. This holy man of God imbued the villagers with the courage to at last stand up to the evil Trenairs."

The smile had gone now. "They were witches every last one of them. And they met the fate they so justly deserved. That is all apart from Molly Trenair who escaped and fled to the New World."

The American laughed. "On her broomstick, I suppose."

The vicar ignored Buchowski's attempt at levity. "All of the Trenairs: man, woman, and child were witches. And that is why you found no Trenairs laid to rest in our graveyard. Such evildoers cannot be buried in consecrated ground." The vicar allowed himself another brief smile. "Not that there was much left of them to be buried."

"Well, that's quite a story, Reverend. I had no idea I was descended from such an infamous family. I sure can't wait to tell everyone back home." Sensing from the silence and unfriendly stares of those in the pub that perhaps he had outstayed his welcome, Buchowski got up to leave. "In fact, it's about time I was on my way. It's quite a trip back to my hotel." He offered his hand to Reverend Dobson. "Well, it was nice meeting you, Reverend."

Reverend Dobson remained in his seat, ignoring Buchowski's proffered hand.

"Well, goodbye then." Buchowski shrugged, and headed towards the door. And to think he had thought these people friendly, he hadn't even had that roast steak he'd been so looking forward to.

Behind him the vicar spoke. "Mr Buchowski! You are a direct descendent of Molly Trenair. And although you bear the name Buchowski, the witch's blood still flows in your veins!"

"He even has the features of a Trenair: the blue eyes, dark hair and large nose," put in one of the old men who had been regaling the American with local gossip earlier.

"Well, excuse me, mister, but it just so happens that those features are prominent on my father's side of the family as well. And it didn't seem to bother you a moment ago."

A group of villagers moved to block his exit.

"Hey, I can assure all you folks, I've never even pulled a rabbit out of a hat; never mind turned anyone into a frog."

"It can be no coincidence that you have come here on the first day of August," said Fred Benton, the landlord.

Buchowski was unsure of the significance. "What on earth's that got to do with anything?"

Benton wasn't convinced. "Ha! He pretends ignorance."

"Lammas, a day when the Trenairs held their foul sabbat," Reverend Dobson enlightened Buchowski.

"George. Ted. Seize him!"

Despite Dobson's sudden order, Buchowski was surprised when the two farmers grabbed him. "Hey, what are you doing? Let me go!" Buchowski was a big man, but he felt sluggish and weak.

He was unable to struggle free. "You put something in my beer!"

"Bring him," commanded the vicar.

The farmers hauled the American out of the pub. The rest of the regulars following.

"Come on, you don't seriously believe in this witchcraft crap, surely? This is the twenty-first century."

"Witchcraft is an evil that must be stamped out, Mr Buchowski, wherever and whenever it is discovered," the vicar answered.

Outside more villagers had gathered. In desperation, Buchowski looked from face to face in the hope that there was someone to whom he could appeal to for aid. But instead, all he saw were expressions of open hostility.

"You guys are crazy!"

Reverend Dobson continued, "However, we are not barbarians, Mr Buchowski. We shall not condemn you out of hand. We shall give you the chance to prove you are free of the taint of the witch blood. There is a tried and trusted method for proving whether one is a witch. If you are as innocent as you proclaim, you will willingly undergo our test."

Still struggling, Buchowski was brought to the edge of the pond. "Where do you guys think you are? This isn't Salem."

"Bring the rope. Tie left foot to right hand; and right foot to left hand."

"Look! I've heard of living history, but this is taking things too far. There's no way I'm agreeing to that," the American protested. "You think I'm crazy? Hell, even I know that that's a no win situation. If I float I'm a witch, and if I don't I drown anyhow."

"On your knees, witch," snarled one of the farmers who held him captive – a ginger-bearded, shaggy-haired fellow.

Buchowski drew on all his reserves of strength. He stamped on the foot of the ginger-bearded farmer, and an elbow in the stomach, winded the other.

And before anyone else could react, Buchowski threw himself into the pond.

Villagers were running around the side of the pond with the intention of surrounding it and him. But the tourist reached the other side before the locals could trap him. He emerged from the pond, wet and slimy. He had lost a sandal, and his camera would be ruined.

Breathing heavily, Buchowski ran as fast as he could, pursued by a baying mob.

He hadn't run as fast since Vietnam. Ahead he could see his hire car – a silver Ford Mondeo. Heart pounding, gasping for breath, Buchowski risked a glance over his shoulder. The villagers were still pursuing him, but he would reach his car before they got to him. He laughed in relief. He was going to make it.

For an agonising moment he thought he had lost the key, but

then he found it, and had started the engine. Buchowski started to accelerate just as the fastest of the pursuing villagers threw himself onto the bonnet of the car. The local managed to hang on for mere seconds before losing his precarious grip. Buchowski sped out of the village, whooping in exhilaration, adrenaline pumping.

The American was driving far too recklessly for such a narrow country road. He was fortunate that he met no other traffic coming in the opposite direction.

His luck ran out whilst he was glancing in the rear-view mirror looking for pursuers. He saw the stray sheep that was in the middle of the road at the last moment. Instinctively he swerved to avoid it. Losing control of the car, the Mondeo went off the road and head-on into a tree. The front of the car crumpled, and Buchowski thanked God for the invention of airbags.

He clambered out of the car. Shaken by the crash and unsteady on his feet. The sheep seemed unperturbed, and was busy grazing the grass verge.

Buchowski swore at the animal. "Damn stupid creature, you're lucky not to be lamb chops!" It must have escaped from the field to the left that contained a flock of Suffolks.

The American wasn't far enough away from the village to be safe; he could see some of the villagers running along the road. And as he watched, a Land Rover sped past them. If he stayed on the road, there was no way he could escape. But if he sought refuge in the wood that grew alongside, well, he just might be able to evade his pursuers.

Yet even as entered the trees he could hear the barking of dogs.

Nettles stung his legs, and thorny briars scratched the American as he pressed deeper into the trees. Buckthorn, hawthorn, rowan and ash made up the bulk of the wood.

Buchowski staggered, wheezing from his exertions. He'd let

himself go, and was out of shape. He hated to admit it, but he was fat not fit. He was an old man in an English wood, not the young soldier he had been in the jungles of Vietnam. An old man who ate, drank and smoked too much, and exercised too little.

The adrenaline rush had worn off. He was getting chest pains, and he'd drunk too much beer too quickly; and he suspected that last pint had been drugged.

Despite his discomfort he kept going. He had to get away. He struggled on, only to trip over a fallen branch. Buchowski landed awkwardly with a cry of pain. He had twisted his ankle.

He tried but hadn't the energy to get up again. "You damn fat old fool," Buchowski swore at himself. And at the villagers, "Bunch of crazy bastards!" What the hell was going on here? Were these people serious? Had he stumbled upon the British equivalent of some inbred, hillbilly rednecks? Or was it one big joke at his expense?

He was afraid, but he wasn't sure which worried him more: the fact that all this might be for real, or that he might be being played for a fool.

He could hear them getting closer, villagers shouting, dogs barking wildly. It wouldn't be long before they found him.

A young woman reached him first, Buchowski realised he recognised her pretty face. She was the barmaid from the pub. She knelt down by the American, and said, "We're not all superstitious yokels, Mr Buchowski. We don't all believe in witchcraft."

Then she was up and away.

Buchowski called, "Hey, don't leave me. Where are you going?" He hoped she had gone to fetch help.

He forced himself up, using the branch to help him rise. But it was too late. The villagers had found him.

"Hey, come on, you guys. You've had your fun. Just let me go and I promise I won't report this to the authorities. I'll forget all this ever happened. And that I ever came to Hexhill."

Reverend Dobson smiled. "I'm sorry, Mr Buchowski, but you have condemned yourself by refusing to take the test."

Buchowski changed his grip on the branch, and held it two-handed, to use it as a club. "In that case you leave me no choice." He swung the branch threateningly. "I'm not afraid to use this."

"And I'm not afraid to use this either." The farmer that Buchowski had earlier elbowed in the stomach was armed with a shotgun, and it was aimed at the American.

"Put the branch down, Mr Buchowski." Reverend Dobson ordered, stepping closer to the tourist, "There can be no escape."

Buchowski's grin was humourless. "Maybe I should go down fighting, Reverend."

The vicar shrugged. "It's your choice."

With a sigh, Buchowski chose to drop the branch; pinning his hopes on the barmaid fetching help. Hell, he wasn't John Wayne. It was unlikely he would even have been able to land one blow, before the farmer shot him.

"A wise decision, Mr Buchowski."

"I hope so," muttered the American.

"I say I should just shoot him anyway." The farmer wasn't so convinced.

"No, Ted, this must be done properly." The vicar exerted his authority.

"Then let's get on with it, Reverend," Ted conceded. "There's harvesting I should be getting on with." Several others murmured agreement.

"Come on, witch." George, the ginger-bearded farmer shoved the American.

"And you can carry this yourself." Benton, the pub landlord, thrust a bundle of wood into the tourist's arms.

"Dear God! You cannot be serious." Buchowski realised what

the villagers had in mind for him.

"Get a move on." Villagers crowded around the American, pushing and shoving, and the limping prisoner was escorted back to the village.

On Hexhill village green, more of the locals had built a bonfire, at the heart of which stood a wooden stake. A man stood ready with a length of rope.

The villagers weren't going to let Buchowski escape again, and they soon had him bound and tied to the stake.

The American clung desperately to the hope that this was some sort of crazy British idea of re-enacting traditional historical events to give tourists a taste of Ye Olde England. Or was some kind of elaborate practical joke being played on him?

Perhaps he had been set up by one of those television programmes, and at the climactic moment the grinning TV host would reveal himself, calling proceedings to a halt.

Whatever it was, it was in very bad taste, and he somehow doubted if he would see the funny side afterwards. In fact, it was entirely possible he would be consulting his lawyer about the situation. But that was what it had to be, they couldn't really intend to burn him at the stake. Could they? Hell, he just didn't know what to think.

Reverend Dobson stepped forward and surveyed the crowd. Then he began to speak, "Does not the Bible say—"

"Wait!" somebody shouted. "Let me through."

Buchowski uttered a prayer of thanks; at last someone had come to put a stop to this madness.

A young woman pushed her way to the front of the crowd. Buchowski heaved a sigh of relief; it was the woman who had whispered to him in the wood – the barmaid. "Oh, thank the Lord. You don't know how glad I am to see you."

The barmaid smiled at Buchowski.

The relief was evident on the American's face. "Ha," he cried, "the police are on their way. You crazy bastards, the police will have you all locked up. You can't treat an American this way and expect to get away with it." A doubt suddenly crossed his mind: surely he should be hearing sirens as the police raced to his rescue. Why wasn't he hearing sirens? "You did get the police? Didn't you?"

In response, she stepped closer to the pyre and spat in his face – much to his shock and the amusement of many in the crowd.

The vicar wasn't one of them. "Really, Miss Benton, there is no need for that sort of behaviour."

"Please carry on, Reverend Dobson," she said, winking at the vicar.

Reverend Dobson coughed, then began his speech again. "Does not the Bible say; *'Thou shall not suffer a witch to live?'*" he asked, his gaze lingering disapprovingly on Abi Benton.

The villagers responded with cries of "Yes!" that were soon followed by shouts of, "Burn the witch!"

Dobson turned to the American. "Therefore, Mr Buchowski, you must meet the same just fate that befell your kin."

The crowd parted again and Fred Benton came forward carrying a burning brand.

Buchowski struggled frantically, but his efforts were useless. The ropes had been tied securely. "For God's sake, you can't mean to go through with this."

Again the American looked from face to face in the desperate hope there was someone who would stop this madness. But the faces of the villagers were countenances of hostility and hatred, mingled with expressions of excitement. Buchowski's worst fears were confirmed. These people were not acting. There was to be no rescue. No television show presenter was going to suddenly emerge from the crowd and stop things in the nick of time. However improbable it seemed: this was for real.

"Reverend Dobson, please have mercy. I'm begging you,

please don't do this."

The vicar nodded to the Mockingbird's landlord. Benton hesitated a moment, mumbling an apology to the vicar for his daughter's behaviour. Then he set the torch to the brushwood at the bottom of the bonfire. The wood was dry and quickly took flame.

The American was weeping now, shaking with fear.

"Oh, God in Heaven, help me! Help me! Please somebody! Help!" he wailed.

Buchowski could feel the heat. The flames were getting closer. Smoke rising, again he screamed for mercy, but the villagers were singing a hymn, and either did not hear, or chose to ignore his pleas.

His cries turned to curses. Thick black smoke choking him, he began to cough. He suffered agonising pain as the flames reached him. But Buchowski continued to curse the villagers for as long as he was able.

However, the American's maledictions did not have the power that those of his ancestors had been purported to have had.

FACE TO FACE

The last thing Dave Brenner saw before he went to sleep was a face.

Although he thought there was something familiar about the face, he did not actually recognise it.

Ordinarily seeing a strange face in your bedroom would perhaps come as something of a shock, especially when there was no evidence of the face being attached to a person. But Brenner had been out on the town, and was by this late hour more than a little drunk. And in the brief moment that this uninvited face registered upon his drink-sodden mind, he gave the matter little attention, and drifted off into slumber.

When Brenner awoke, a little after two o'clock the following afternoon, he had forgotten all about the advent of the strange visage. His immediate concern was the pounding in his head, and the fact that he had gone to bed alone. That was something of a rarity.

After showering, Brenner preened himself, studying his reflection in the bathroom mirror. So absorbed was he with his handsome features, and perfecting his hairstyle, that it was some moments before he realised that reflected beside his own was another face.

"What the …?" he muttered, then span round, saying, "Who's that? What do you want?" as he did so.

Brenner grunted. To his surprise, he found that he was alone. He turned back to look in the mirror, this time to see only his own image. He shrugged his shoulders and said to his reflection, "Seeing things, you wanna watch that, me old son. Next thing you know, you'll be talking to yourself."

"Good stuff this, Paul." Brenner passed the joint to his friend. Paul inhaled deeply. "Sure is," he agreed.

"'Ere, what happened to you last night?" Paul asked. "You losing your touch, or something?"

"Nah," Brenner sneered. "That place was full of lesbians."

"Ah."

"You going to the Goat tonight?" Brenner asked.

"Dunno. You?"

"Course I am."

"'Ere, what you got to eat?" Paul suddenly asked. "I could do with some munchies."

"Yeah, me too," Brenner agreed. "I'll see what I can find in the kitchen, you roll another one up." But he made no move to rise from where he sprawled on the couch.

"Sure thing, man." Paul giggled, "Shit, listen to me, I sound like some bleedin' old hippie."

Brenner started to get up. "Cheeky bastard!" he suddenly exclaimed.

"You what?" Paul asked, confused.

"There's someone at the window."

"What do you mean, there's someone at the window?"

Brenner was crossing the room. "I don't know who 'e is, but I've seen 'im before."

"Dave, man, there's no one at the window, you're hallucinating." Paul remained lying on the floor, his eyes closed, and feeling rather pleased with himself for managing to pronounce hallucinating correctly first time.

"Don't be daft, dope don't make you hallucinate," Brenner snorted.

Paul glanced at his friend. "Who you calling a dope?"

Brenner ignored him.

The face was peering through the window. There was something indistinct about it, but Brenner knew it was grinning, laughing at him.

"Oi! What the bleedin' 'ell do you think you're playing at?" Brenner shouted.

Halfway across the room, he suddenly stopped. "Hang on ..." he muttered. It was impossible that someone could be at his window. This was a block of flats, and he lived on the tenth floor!

"Bloody window cleaners," he swore, covering the rest of the distance.

"What the fuck?" Brenner opened the window, leaned out, and looked up and down. "There's nobody there."

No face, no window cleaners, nothing.

"See, I told you so." Paul said, sagely.

"But I saw it," Brenner protested.

"Nah mate, it was probably a balloon."

Brenner took one last look out of the window, and shook his head. "Yeah, I guess it must have been,"

"C'mon Dave," Paul urged. "Hurry up with that food."

"Yeah all right." Brenner closed the window, and went to the kitchen.

"And bring us another beer, will yah?" Paul called after him.

As was usual on a Saturday night, the Capering Goat was packed. A crowd of young men and women, some of them looking for a sexual partner, some merely to get drunk, many seeking to do both. Those who had not succeeded in pulling come closing time would move on to a nightclub to continue their quest.

Paul had not turned up, but Brenner sat at a table with another of his friends. Brenner knew many of the people there, but he caught a glimpse of someone lurking behind a couple of the regulars, that made him stare. It was the face he had seen previously.

Brenner pointed. "'Ere Darren who's that?" he asked his companion.

"Who?"

"Over there, behind Fat John, and Mickey Sykes."

Darren peered in their direction. "What you on about, Dave? There's no one else there."

"What do you mean no one else there? Of course there's someone there. You going blind or something?"

Darren glared at his friend. "It's you that needs your eyes testing," he said, getting up, and taking his pint with him.

"Oi, Darren!" Brenner called after him. "Where you going? It's your round."

Darren ignored him, and disappeared into the crowd.

"Bollocks!" muttered Brenner. He drained his pint and made his way to the bar.

"Another one in there, please, darling."

"Is there something the matter, Dave?" Shirley, the barmaid asked.

"No. Why?"

"Oh I dunno, you seem distracted."

"To tell the truth I think someone's following me."

Shirley leaned closer; Brenner eyed her cleavage appreciatively.

"What, you mean like a stalker or something?" she asked.

"Nah."

"Oh." Shirley sounded disappointed. "Here, hang on a minute, I've got to ring for last orders."

The resulting charge to the bar kept Shirley busy, but Brenner took every opportunity to use his charms on the blonde barmaid. And all thoughts of the mysterious face were forgotten as the more important pursuits of a young man on a Saturday night out took precedence.

Brenner's efforts paid off.

"Fancy coming back to mine?" Shirley asked him when the rush ended.

Brenner grinned; he had obviously been right about the women he had tried to chat up the previous night. Real women still fell at his feet.

Her eyes closed, face contorted, Shirley gasped and moaned as she rode Brenner's penis. He loved to watch her breasts bouncing up and down, and the expressions upon her face.

"Talk dirty to me," she gasped.

"You dirty slut!" Brenner grunted. "I'm gonna fuck your brains out, you filthy bitch!"

"Oh yeah, fuck me hard, you bastard!" she responded, his crude words encouraging her to wilder exertions, and her cries grew louder.

"Oh God!" he gasped. "I'm gonna cum!" But at the height of their passion, Brenner was distracted from Shirley's bouncing breasts by the sudden looming appearance of someone peering over her shoulder. Brenner's cry was close to a scream - a mixture of ecstasy mingled with shock.

Normally the idea of an audience would have added to his sexual pleasure, but – in reality – when it was a disembodied face that haunted him, it was a different matter.

"Dave, lover, are you all right?" Shirley panted.

"Yeah," he gasped. "It's just that I thought there was someone watching us."

"You what?" Shirley quickly covered herself with a bed sheet. "What do you mean someone watching?"

"It's all right, they've gone."

"You bloody well make sure," she said, shoving him out of bed. "I don't want no bloody perverts spying on me."

Brenner made a thorough search of Shirley's flat, but there was no trace of the intruder.

Brenner sat on the edge of the bed, and lit a cigarette. He took a drag, then passed it to Shirley. "You remember I was telling you I thought someone was following me?"

"Yeah, you didn't tell me it was some pervert though."

"It's not. At least, I don't think it is."

"Then who is it? What do they want?"

"I dunno."

"You should tell the police."

"No way, they'd never believe me."

"Why wouldn't't they?"

He grunted. "I doubt even you would believe me."

"Try me."

"It's not a person," he began.

"Not a person? What do you mean?"

Brenner hesitated, unsure whether to go on.

"Dave? What is it?"

Brenner sighed. "It's a face."

"What do you mean, a face?"

"I keep seeing this face. There's something familiar about it, but I can't put a name to it."

"Well why don't you ask them who they are and what they want?"

"If only it was as simple as that. This face, Shirl', it's not right."

"Not right?"

"It's deformed. No, that's not right. It's more like it hasn't had time to properly develop yet. I can never make out its features clearly. I couldn't make out its eyes, but it *was* watching us. And more than that, it's just a face; it's got no body. It just floats there."

"You what?"

Brenner hung his head. "See, I knew you wouldn't believe me."

Shirley stubbed out her cigarette. "I never said I didn't believe you."

Brenner looked at her. "No?"

"No." Smiling, Shirley reached out to him, letting the sheet that covered her, slip from her breasts. "But I seem to remember you saying something about fucking my brains out."

Brenner's relationship with Shirley turned out to be a short-lived affair. Normally it was Brenner who ended a relationship, but in this instance it was Shirley that did so. The end came on their first date proper – a trip to the cinema.

Brenner settled back in his seat, and put his arm around Shirley. She leaned her head against him.

This was a film he had been looking forward to watching. But after a few minutes he rubbed his eyes – it did not help. There was something wrong with the lead actor's face.

"I thought whatshisname was supposed to be in this," he whispered to Shirley.

"Whatshisname? That is whatshisname, as you put it, don't you know anything?" Shirley replied.

Several people went, "*Shush!*"

"Then what's wrong with his face? Is he wearing a mask?" To Brenner it appeared that the indistinct features of the strange face that haunted him had replaced those of the handsome movie star.

"What you on about Dave? I thought you wanted to see this film."

"I do."

"Then shut up and watch it."

"Hear, hear," a member of the audience muttered.

Brenner groaned. As the film progressed, the faces of the cast changed, one by one, into the same half-formed features.

"What's wrong with you?" Shirley whispered.

"Don't you see?"

"See what?"

"There's something wrong with their faces," Brenner insisted.

"Don't you see it? Don't any of you see it?" he said, looking around the darkened cinema.

More shushing ensued.

Embarrassed, Shirley sighed, and sank lower in her seat. Brenner kept his eyes closed for the rest of the film, even during the blockbuster's noisy and spectacular climax.

The film finished and Brenner could not wait to get out of the cinema. "C'mon I need a drink," he said, heading towards the nearest pub.

"You're not the only one," Shirley agreed.

Shirley put down her glass of white wine. "Are you going to tell me what that was all about?" she asked.

But Brenner's attention was elsewhere.

"Dave? Dave?" Shirley shook his arm, but Brenner continued to stare across the barroom. Angry, she suddenly slapped his face.

"What the 'ell was that for?" Brenner asked, rubbing his cheek.

"Don't pretend you don't know, you sod. I saw you."

"Saw me what?" he asked in all innocence.

"You were stood right in front of me, blatantly eyeing up some tart. Couldn't keep your eyes off her."

"No I wasn't. I saw it again," he explained.

"Saw what again?"

"The face."

Shirley was dismissive. "Oh come off it, Dave; there is no face."

"But I'm telling you there is."

"There's only you who's seen it; why is that Dave?"

Brenner grabbed Shirley's arm, spinning her round. "Look over there, see for yourself."

The face hovered in the air; its features seemed to be evolving, becoming clearer. The eyes were staring at him, burning with malevolence.

"There," he pointed. "Don't you see it?" he cried in desperation.

Shirley struggled. "Let go of me! There's nothing there."

Brenner realised that people were starting to stare at them, and he released his hold. No one else appeared to have noticed the face.

Shirley shook her head. "You're mad you are, Dave Brenner. And not only that, you can consider yourself dumped!" She picked up her glass and chucked what was left of the wine in Brenner's face, then stormed out of the pub.

Brenner slumped into a seat, his head in his hands.

Perhaps he was going mad. Seeing a face that no one else could see was bad enough. But a face that was incomplete and yet seemed familiar was another matter entirely. And on top of that, the face wasn't even attached to a body. And always it seemed to be laughing at him – not in good humour, but in a mocking, malicious way.

Finishing his pint, Brenner glanced around him. "Nooo!" he moaned. He saw the same half-formed features wherever he looked.

Avoiding looking at people, he hurried out of the pub and headed homewards; head down, keeping his eyes fixed on where he walked.

At Patel's off-licence, he stopped and went in.

"A bottle of whisky."

"Anything in particular?" the shopkeeper asked. "We have a wide selection."

"One of them litre ones." Brenner would not meet Mr Patel's gaze.

"*Bells*?" the Asian asked.

"Yeah that'll do."

"That will be sixteen pounds and ninety-nine pence please."

"Don't bother with a bag." Brenner handed over two ten-pound notes, but did not wait for his change.

Back in his flat, he poured a full glass of whiskey, drank it down, then repeated the process.

"Right, let's see you." He steeled himself.

Unsure whether he would see the face reflected beside his own image, or his own features replaced by it, Brenner stepped in front of the mirror.

His own face stared back at him – no transformation had taken place, no disembodied face floated next to his.

Brenner's mobile rang. He snatched it up.

"Yes?" he snapped.

A woman's voice asked, "Dave, is that you?"

"Uh huh."

"It's me, Mary … Remember?"

It must have been eight, maybe nine months, but sure he remembered. Mary Campbell. Surprisingly, considering there were so many of them, he never forgot his conquests. In an instant Brenner had conjured up her image in his mind. Long strawberry blonde hair, pretty, green eyes, cute little nose, and luscious lips. And what a body - very fit. But then they all were, Brenner had his standards - he never slept with mingers.

Mary was speaking. "You've seen it too, haven't you?" There was a pleading quality to her voice.

Brenner grunted, "Yes."

"What did it look like?" she asked; her voice had dropped almost to a whisper.

But before Brenner could reply, Mary cried, "The eyes, what were the eyes like?"

"Green," he answered. He groaned. "Like yours."

Mary laughed. "Like mine. Yes, I thought so."

"I'm glad you see the funny side," Brenner snapped.

Mary's laugh became more hysterical. "Actually, no, Dave, I

don't see. But do you?"

"What? No I don't, Mary. What is this? I don't know how you've done it, but if this is your idea of some sort of revenge …"

Mary interrupted him, "It's our child, Dave. What it would look like if it had been born. If it had lived. It has the features of its parents – my eyes. What has it got of yours?"

At a loss for words, Brenner caught sight of his reflection in the mirror, and saw there was something dreadfully wrong. He would have screamed – but he no longer had a mouth.

Another reflection appeared beside his in the mirror. The face had grown more distinctive – Mary's green eyes glared at him, and contorted into a leering sneer was Brenner's own grinning mouth. And for the first time Brenner could hear the laughter that he had always associated with the face.

Brenner threw his phone at the mirror, shattering the glass. And amongst the turmoil of thoughts that raced through his mind, one question of startling clarity abruptly pushed its way to the fore – whose nose would it have?

THE COUGHING COFFIN

"Curious business," muttered Major Guthrie.

And we waited, unsure whether he was addressing us – or merely talking to himself, which was often the Major's wont.

I should say that we were: Dr John Hurst, Edgar Soames, and myself, George Janders. We four – along with the hovering steward, Dawson – were the only chaps who remained at the club that Halloween night. We were comfortably seated in leather armchairs, enjoying some of the finest alcoholic beverages that Dawson could supply us with.

Major Guthrie said nothing further for what must have been five minutes, by which time we had assumed – somewhat disappointedly – that the old boy had merely been commenting aloud on some private reminiscence, and was not about to relate one of his many unusual anecdotes of which he had such a hoard. For in truth, we three had remained at the club, in hopeful anticipation that the Major would recount a suitable tale for the night in question.

"Curious business," he suddenly said again.

Unable to contain myself any longer, I asked, "What was?"

"What?" the Major spluttered. My question had apparently startled him.

"Sorry, Major, but I, well, all three of us actually, were curious about this curious business you keep mentioning, as it were."

"Curious business?" the Major said for a third time, although this time as a question rather than a statement.

Soames opened his mouth, obviously about to prompt the Major.

But before Edgar could speak, Major Guthrie did. "Oh, so you know about it as well, do you?"

"Oh, for goodness sake." Hurst was becoming frustrated. Although he was already in somewhat of a bad mood as I had beaten him in several games of billiards earlier that evening.

"Actually, no, we don't," I said patiently, "but I'm sure we would all like to hear about it."

Edgar and John murmured their agreement.

Major Guthrie consulted his watch. "Well, the tale's not long in the telling."

Hurst breathed a sigh of relief. I, however, was not so convinced by Guthrie's statement.

Although the Major's anecdotes are always interesting to hear, it can be a somewhat trying experience, as the old fellow can be a trifle long-winded. However, I do have my suspicions that the Major isn't as vague as he sometimes appears to be.

"You fellows, no doubt would like to hear it?" he said at last.

Again, we murmured our agreement.

Major Guthrie signalled to the club steward. "Ah, Dawson. Another scotch and soda. Put it on George's account, would you? There's a good fellow."

As I had said, I had beaten Hurst at billiards that night, winning a tidy sum in the process, so I indicated that Dawson should bring more drinks for all of us.

And once Dawson had done so, Major Guthrie began his story.

"Well now, it so happened back in eighty-four, that I was staying up in, in ... um ... ah ..." Guthrie paused trying to recall where exactly he had been staying. "Well, remote sort of a place, wherever it was. I was up – yes, it was definitely up – up there doing a spot of hunting and shooting, and what have you, you know the sort of thing, I'm sure?" The Major raised a querying eyebrow.

We nodded and agreed that we did indeed.

"Anyway, it wasn't there, wherever that was, but at a place called Morstan House that the events in my story took place. Do you know it?" Guthrie asked.

We didn't.

"Well, my old regimental comrade, Hadingly-Scott had got

the place, and he'd invited me to visit if I was ever in the locale. I can't for the life of me think why, as we could never stand each other. But there you are, and so, as it were, was I. You see this hunting and shooting trip that I had taken, was indeed in the locale of Morstan House. Wherever that might in fact be. Tricky thing memory, you see. Has this strange habit of playing tricks on you," he offered by way of explanation of his memory loss.

"Well, I turned up unannounced and unexpected at Morstan House, and was horrified to find that Hadingly-Scott had passed away. Terrible loss, really fine fellow. I must have missed hearing about his death because I had been out of the country at the time. But I can't tell you anything about that – top-secret, don't you know? And to think no one bothered to inform me!" the Major snorted in disgust.

"I did remember that before I had left for India, I had heard that Hadingly-Scott had not long returned from someplace in Africa, and was suffering from some sort of illness – but I had no idea that it might have been serious. Furthermore, there had been a number of rumours doing the rounds. Rumours that he had had some sort of falling out with one of those witch doctor fellows whilst he was over there."

Seemingly unaware that he had let slip that his top-secret mission had taken him to India the Major leaned forward conspiratorially. "Apparently this falling out resulted in the witch doctor putting some sort of curse on old Hadingly-Scott. Would you believe it?"

"Mumbo jumbo." Hurst snorted.

"You think so, do you, Doctor?" Guthrie sat back in his chair, and paused to light a cigar. "Ah, that's good," he declared.

John remained sceptical. "Superstitious nonsense."

Major Guthrie raised an eyebrow at John's scepticism. "Queer sorts those witch doctor chaps; don't you know? I remember back in seventy-nine; when I was out in Africa myself," the

Major paused again, a pained expression upon his face. "Actually, now I come to mention it, I don't remember. How extraordinary. Oh well, never mind."

I had to smile, as I heard poor old Hurst groan. Fortunately, the Major didn't notice.

"Anyway, where was I? Oh, yes." Picking up the thread of his story again, the Major continued. "So his son was master of Morstan House now, and although the fellow was obviously still in mourning, and had a quite distressed and distracted air, he invited me in and made me most welcome.

"We dined on a simply excellent dinner, absolutely splendid meal." The Major patted his belly. And I feared we were in for a discourse on food – one of the Major's favourite topics.

Obviously I was not alone in my fears because Soames asked, "Did you broach the subject of Hadingly-Scott senior's death?"

That earned him a glare from the Major, but I'm sure Edgar thought it was worth it.

"Of course I enquired about the manner of his father's death, but perhaps not surprisingly he was reluctant to talk about his father's demise in depth. However, he did reveal that it was true that his father had succumbed to an illness he had picked up whilst on the Dark Continent. I'm a sensitive sort of chap, so I did not press him for more details."

The Major took a mouthful of his drink.

"Naturally, I thought it only right that I should pay my respects to old Hadingly-Scott."

The Major broke off from his story. "See to the fire would you, Dawson?"

The steward hastened to obey.

"I don't know much about architecture, so I couldn't tell you when Morstan House was built, but it's enough to say that it's an old place. Old enough to have one of those private chapels adjoining the house," the Major explained.

"Hadingly-Scott had been laid to rest in its crypt, and after

68

dinner I ventured down to this underground vault to pay my respects to the old fellow.

"You'd think it wouldn't affect an old soldier like myself – must have faced death a hundred times or more. But I have to admit, I found it quite an unnerving experience, being underground in this ill-lit sepulchre, surrounded by all these boxes containing the remains of long dead people. Made me contemplate the fact that that's the fate that awaits us all. But I don't suppose you young fellows ever bother to think about your own mortality."

Rather unusually for the Major, he did not wait for us to reply. He had evidently warmed to his tale.

"Now, neither young Hadingly-Scott nor a servant had accompanied me down to the vault, and I thought I was quite alone down there. But I realised that that was not the case when I quite distinctly heard someone cough.

"I glanced around but could see no one. The cough had definitely come from inside the crypt, and I called out, 'Who's there?' No one answered, but then I heard the coughing again.

"At first, I had thought it was the cough of someone trying to attract my attention – and perhaps the first time it was. But I realised that it was the cough of someone suffering from some sort of malady.

"Well, despite my discomfort, I knew I would have to look further into the crypt. I had to know if someone needed aid, or whether it was someone's idea of a joke."

"Rather bad taste," said Soames.

"Yes, quite," the Major agreed.

"So there I was, just preparing myself to delve deeper when a voice spoke. 'You hear it too.' It was young Hadingly-Scott, although at first I didn't really pay attention to the words that he had said. Made me jump, you see, I'd been sure I was alone.

"'Damn it all, Hadingly-Scott,' I said, 'I didn't realise you were in here with me. You ought to get something for that cough of yours.' Well, the fellow just stared at me, and it suddenly dawned on me, what he had actually said.

"And whilst he stared at me, I heard again that pitiful coughing. And I finally realised where it was coming from. Yes, gentlemen, from the senior Hadingly-Scott's coffin!"

"My God!" exclaimed Soames.

"Catalepsy!" gasped Dr Hurst.

"Buried alive," I said. "The poor fellow."

"Monstrous!" I heard Dawson cry.

Hurst shook his head. "It's like something that fellow Poe would have written."

The Major was indignant at our quite understandable – I thought – interruption. "Am I telling this story or not?" He huffed.

We profusely agreed that he indeed was, and urged him to continue. Soames even had Dawson fetch the Major another drink to placate him.

"Well, if you chaps would let me get on with it, rather than interrupting all the time, you would learn that it is a tale more strange than you imagine."

The Major had a slight smile of amusement – I noted now – but I don't think any of the others noticed.

He continued, "Overcoming my initial shock, I realised why the junior Hadingly-Scott had been so reticent over the manner of his father's death. And quite naturally I suspected some sort of foul play on his part."

"Quite naturally," echoed Hurst.

"I demanded that the coffin be opened immediately. The heir sighed, but agreed that it would be so. He called for a servant and instructed him.

"One by one the nails were drawn out. So painstakingly slowly, that in frustration I took over, levering the lid off, myself."

Eagerly we leaned forward in our seats, and Dawson loitered

near at hand, anxious to hear the denouement to the Major's story.

"You gentlemen speak of Edgar Allan Poe, and his story of premature burial, ah, what a hideous fate to be buried alive." Major Guthrie shuddered at the thought, as I suspect did we all.

"And indeed the coughing coming from that coffin had installed the thought in my mind that that was the very fate that had befallen dear old Hadingly-Scott."

Major Guthrie paused. I am still unsure whether it was because of the enormity of what he was about to reveal, or whether he was merely savouring the expectant expressions on the faces of his rapt audience.

I could stand the suspense no longer, and neither evidently could John. "Well?" he prompted before I could.

Guthrie finished his drink and nodded. "But you see gentlemen, the body contained in his coffin was quite unmistakably dead, and had clearly been so for quite some time!"

And with much shaking of heads, we all had to agree that it was indeed a curious business.

THE MADNESS OUT OF THE SEA

It began with a pounding upon the church door and a cry, "Open up. Open up for pity's sake!"

Roused from my prayers I hastened to open the door – to reveal an old man. A man lean of limb and gaunt of face. With wild hair, unkempt and white, and a face pocked and scarred. His clothes were worn and dirty, and he smelt strongly of alcohol.

"Sanctuary, I demand sanctuary," he gasped, collapsing to his knees. He wrapped his arms around my legs, and, wheezing as if after a strenuous run, he begged, "For the love of God, grant me sanctuary, Father!"

At any moment I expected to see a mob of pursuers come charging along the road, for he had the appearance of a man chased by Satan's very hounds of hell.

But there was no one else to be seen. Just this ragged old man, and his much-travelled haversack.

"Have you a bed for an old man?" he asked. "It'll be a bitterly cold night, Father, and there's a storm coming. I can feel it, don't you know?"

I must admit I was rather taken aback by his request and his actions. Did he seek sanctuary or merely accommodation? I looked up at the sky – it was blue with a few white clouds. There was no indication of a storm brewing.

"Have you not tried the village inn?" I asked, indicating Kirowan's pub.

"As they say, there's no room at the inn. Besides I'd rather spend the night here in the church or under the roof of a man of God." He released his hold on my legs and clasped his hands together.

"I'd feel safer – for I'd dare say the inn is full of rogues, and if the Lord cannot protect me from those others, then no one can," he said cryptically.

"Surely you can find room for me," he went on. "Or is there no such thing as Christian charity anymore?"

"Have you broken the law, my son? Are the authorities seeking you?"

"You must hear my confession," was his reply. "I am not long for this world," he muttered, as he rose from his knees.

"God welcomes those who are prepared to repent of their sins, my son." I told him piously, allowing him to enter.

"Like as not, you'll not believe me, but I swear to you, Father, that it's the God's honest truth, no word of a lie."

His shirt was ragged and so faded that I could not be sure what colour it had once been. A man obviously fallen on hard times. I could see tattoos on his arms. "You're a sailor," I guessed.

"Aye, Father, you're right at that. Patrick Crawford is my name."

"You're aways from the sea."

"Not far *enough*, Father." He shuddered, then muttered again, "not far enough," looking around the church, as if there were someone or perhaps something hidden, about to pounce upon him.

"Oh?" I was, I admit, curious.

He seemed satisfied that we were alone, and he sat down on a pew. "A sailor, yes, and I've sailed all over. But I'll never go near the sea again."

And so Crawford began to recount a most remarkably wicked tale of a life of sin.

"I've sailed the seven seas, Father, travelled far and wide. Been to some strange places, too, the Americas, Africa, and the Indies, the Near East, and the far reaches of the Orient. And, believe me; I've seen some strange things in my time. But none so strange as that last time in the South Seas.

"I was serving on board the brig *Mary-Anne* at the time."

I interrupted, "Perhaps we should move to the confessional,

74

Mr Crawford."

But the old sailor ignored my suggestion, so I seated myself, content to listen to his story. I must admit I am somewhat partial to a good yarn.

"We'd had a successful trip trading among the islands of the South Pacific, when we were hit by the storm. It came on all of sudden, no warning. One moment we're sailing along, perfect conditions, and then *whoosh*, it hits us. Unnatural, it were. Now I've seen some storms in my time, but *this* one, I've never seen the like before.

"Terrible, it were. Almost, you could say, of biblical proportions. Neptune were in a right temper."

Recalling where he was, and who he was talking to, the old sailor coughed. "Er, pardon me, Father, rather I mean God was."

I nodded and indicated that he should continue.

"A roaring tempest, it was. The storm raged, the ship was tossed about, the sails were torn and the masts broken. We was taking on water, and men were being washed overboard. The ship was doomed." The seaman paused momentarily, shaking his head, remembering what would have been a truly terrifying experience.

"It was a storm that by rights no one should have survived. But somehow, three of us did. As well as myself, there was the ship's cook, a Lascar by the name of Ali – to tell the truth I'm not even sure that Ali was his real name, but it's what everyone called him nevertheless – and a deck hand, a Cornish man called Jake Webster. Just the three of us, all adrift in this little boat.

"The storm had passed, but there was no sign of any other lifeboats, or any wreckage. And, for all I know, we were the only ones that had survived.

"But how we were still alive and not drowned, or ended up as some shark's dinner, I do not know. A miracle, I suppose that's what it was, a bloody miracle. Thank the Lord.

"We drifted for days – I lost count of how many. It seemed endless at the time. Nothing but us and the sea. We had run out of food and fresh water when we finally sighted land. We were delirious by then, and thought it was a hallucination. For there should have been no islands in those parts, unless we were even farther off course than we thought. Besides, we did not have the strength to even try and paddle our way to it.

"But luck was with us, and the current took us in the right direction, and we washed up on the beach. Although at the time, I had the strangest feeling that someone, or rather some*thing*, was swimming alongside us, guiding our course. At the time, I put that down to my poor condition. Although, now, I'm not so sure my first impression was not correct."

Again the old sailor became briefly distant, lost in his memories. I waited patiently, and before long, Crawford resumed his story.

"Anyhow, as I say, we washed up on this beach, and mighty relieved we were to find that it was a real island. We staggered out of the boat, unsteady on our legs after all that time in our little craft. And all of a sudden there are these people coming down to the beach. Well, we were a bit worried like, 'cause sometimes some of the tribes you get on these islands are pretty savage. And really, we were in no fit state for a fight.

"But I still had my cutlass, and Ali his favourite meat cleaver, that he had somehow held onto despite everything. And young Jake was a big lad, and pretty handy with his fists.

"But would you believe it, we needn't have been so worried. You see these islanders were all women. Beautiful, dusky maidens. And, boy, did they make us welcome! Couldn't do enough for us, treated us like kings! Let's just say they were real friendly like, if you get my meaning, Father." For a moment, I thought the sailor was going to have the audacity to wink at me, instead he grinned lewdly.

76

"Didn't speak a word of English, though, but it didn't matter. I mean, if they had, you can bet, as I told Jake, that it wouldn't be long before they'd start nagging us. Anyhow, they seemed to know whatever we wanted, whenever we wanted it."

Despite my frown, the mariner's grin grew broader.

"My dreams had come true, although I suppose part of me did not really believe it was real. I had been studying the positions of the stars, but they did not make sense. Their alignments were all wrong, and they were wildly different each night. I thought it was a dream and that I was still really drifting at sea in that little lifeboat, or maybe I was dead, and gone to Heaven. Where were their men folk? I wondered but never really let it concern me. Here we were on this luxurious tropical island surrounded by beautiful, willing, subservient women.

"We all had our favourites among the women. I was particularly fond of a real beauty whose name was Nia. Long, dark tresses, lovely blue eyes, and a perfect smile. And what a body!" the old sailor sketched a figure with his hands.

Finally realising I was frowning; he hurried on with his tale.

"We must have spent a fortnight there, by which time we had well and truly recovered from our ordeal. I don't think any of us had thoughts of leaving. It was Paradise, you see." He sighed, "Little did we know that we were soon to leave our Garden of Eden and go to Hell.

"On what was to turn out to be our last night on the island, the women held some kind of religious ceremony. Unexpectedly, afterwards there was another terrible storm akin to the one that had wrecked the *Mary-Anne*.

"I'd noticed that, during the ceremony, some of the women wore exotic jewellery – Nia among them – and naturally I was curious as to how they had come by it.

"I managed to make my interest clear to Nia, and she indicated that it had come from another island. That news took me by surprise. There were no other islands visible from our side of the island, and neither myself, Ali or Jake, had bothered to explore very far inland. Life, ye see, was far too pleasurable for us to bother with such things. The possibility that there were other islands beyond this one hadn't even occurred to us.

"Of course, I indicated that I wanted to be taken there. And like everything else I had wanted since landing on the island, my wish was granted.

"The storm raged long into the night, and I feared the village would be blown away. But the next day dawned bright and clear. The sea was calm, and, remarkably, the village was undamaged.

"I had not expected that everyone from the village would set off in a flotilla of canoes to this other island. I had not even intended telling Ali or Jake what I planned.

"And so it was that our stay in Paradise came to an end.

"This other island was farther away than I had expected, and I dozed on the voyage, as must have Ali and Jake.

"When Nia roused me, we had arrived. It was clear that we were on a very different island. I have already said that, by rights, there didn't ought to be any islands in those waters, and where they took us to, didn't ought to exist anywhere.

"I think all three of us sensed that this was a bad place to be. I suppose we should have got in one of the canoes and left straight away, but no one wanted to let on how scared he was. Besides, there was the lure of finding some of that jewellery of such strange design. And the women were eager to show us this new island, urging us on."

I was taken aback by Crawford's sudden wail. "How could we have known they were those sirens of the old sea legends?" The sailor's expression was genuinely pained.

I began to point out that he should have been all too aware of the treacherous nature of the seductress, but he forestalled me. "No sermons, please, Father."

78

I had already realised he was not really making a confession in the traditional sense, so I acquiesced. "Very well. Tell me about this island. If I understand you right, it is this island that you mean to liken to hell itself."

He took a moment to compose himself before continuing. "I been in some queer places, believe me. But this island – who would have thought it possible? There was a city of sorts, but them buildings were all wrong. Built of obsidian, and basalt, even some of coral, and a strange green stone, the like of which I ain't never seen before.

"It's hard to explain. I mean, there were bits that reminded me of them pyramids like what they have in Egypt. And in parts, it reminded me of some of them queer temples they have in India.

"We wandered around in silent awe, unable to believe our eyes. There was something not right about them buildings. They didn't seem to fit together quite right, if you get my meaning? No, of course you wouldn't … It was all real confusing. Maybe I wasn't as recovered as I had thought. Maybe I was suffering some sort of delusions brought on by my ordeal of drifting at sea.

"The angles were wrong, and you could never be sure how big they were really. Some seemed smaller inside than they should have been, whilst others had rooms that were so big they should not have fit inside the walls that contained them.

"There were minarets and spires, and such like. Oh, it were mighty strange, especially all them queer statues.

"They was like them heathen Egyptian gods, part man and part animal. Their bodies were like that of a man but with a pair of wings upon the back. And for a head, an octopus of some kind. Hideous, yet the women regarded them with great reverence.

"There was something else equally disturbing that I noticed. Despite the warmth of the sun, the buildings were all wet.

"There were crustaceans of barnacles and things. And

everything was covered in seaweed and wrack. Puddles of seawater teemed with fish, crabs and other such creatures from the deeps.

"I had no doubt that this island had not long before been beneath the sea, and had risen from the deeps only recently. Who knows, it may have been drowned Atlantis, and maybe it weren't. The sea's claimed more than one place for its own.

"Although I had assumed the island was uninhabited, I soon learned that I was wrong.

"We heard them before we saw them. Drawn by the beating of drums, and the wailing sound of horns fashioned from conch shells, we discovered that the unnatural buildings were as nothing as to those that lived in them.

"They were men, I suppose," Crawford shuddered, "at least some of them were. But they were the ugliest race of men I have ever seen. Their features reminded me of fish, frogs, seals and turtles. They had scaly skin, greyish-green in colour. And the bulging eyes, and gills, Father." The old sailor was becoming agitated.

"Most had gangling arms that ended in webbed hands. But some had tentacles instead of arms. I swear!" Crawford had risen and was pacing around now.

"They were bad enough, but worst of them all was—" Suddenly the mariner wailed. "God help me, but it should not have been possible. Father, he was at least eight feet tall, and he wore yellow robes and a real fancy crown on his octopus head. I think he was their king, or maybe their high priest."

"Octopus head?"

"That's right, Father." He grasped hold of me; put his face close to mine. Madness shone in his eyes, but I managed not to recoil from him. "Eight slimy tentacles protruded from his hideous face. Imagine it, Father. Just imagine it!"

Abruptly his mood changed. He loosed his grip and stepped back. He looked at me slyly. "You don't believe me, do you?"

Suddenly, he reached for his bag and rummaged around in it. After a moment he pulled out a bundle wrapped in a piece of tattered yellow cloth. "Well, just you take a look at this then," he said, unwrapping the bundle to reveal an ostentatious piece of jewellery.

It was a crown of sorts, tall, and bejewelled with a mixture of pearls and diamonds, and a jade figure of some loathsome octopoid idol.

I had never seen the like before, and it occurred to me that it would take great skill to wear it balanced upon the head.

"Here," my guest said, "you're a priest – you try it on." Reluctantly, I tried to do so, and I could not get it to sit right. It was as if it had been specially designed for a particular person, an individual with a most peculiarly shaped head indeed.

"You see?" Crawford said eagerly.

"It's an unusual piece, I'll admit." But it did not mean his story was true. Yet, on the other hand, where else could he have got it from?

I studied the crown closely. I am no expert, but it certainly appeared to me that it was of great value. But as I did so, I shuddered. I suddenly felt quite repelled by the item. I knew without question that it was unwholesome, and I quickly handed it back.

"It is an evil thing, my son," I told him. "You would do well to be rid of it." I was quite relieved when Crawford covered it again, and returned it to his haversack. He then sat down again and continued his tale.

"It was plain that there was a ceremony going on. But it weren't orderly, like your Catholic ceremonies. No sir, Father, it was a racket of grunting and croaking, squawking, groaning, howling, screeching, shrieking, yelping and baying. A right awful din that no man should have to hear. Yet, I still hear it, when they are close."

Crawford paused in his narration to listen. "They are coming for me. They are coming for me!"

"Calm down, my son. No one can take you from God's holy house. You are safe here."

Eventually he grew calmer and I asked him to recommence his account of what happened on that strange South Sea island.

"When they spotted us, they fell silent. Then a group of them came to meet us. And we were escorted into the heart of this weird gathering.

"I said that the maidens of the first island could not speak English. But they sure could communicate with this bunch. We watched, and they bowed full length on the ground before these Atlantis folk, or whatever they were. Reluctantly, we knew we better do likewise."

"Atlanteans," I said.

"Eh?" Crawford frowned at the unfamiliar word.

"If this was indeed Atlantis – and that name will suffice for want of another – they would be Atlanteans," I explained.

"Oh, right. Well, whatever they were, the priest-king motioned for us to rise, and then beckoned my Nia forward. Already shocked by what we had seen, we were in for a further surprise when we realised what was in store for us.

"Obediently she went to him, then knelt before him. Again she was commanded to rise. And then this priest or king, whatever he was, reached out and caressed her with his arm. It moved like a snake, like it had no bones! First it touched her face, and then her body. I knew what their priest-king intended. Can you believe the disgust I felt, Father?"

He did not wait for me to reply.

"Well, it got lots worse once I saw that Nia was more than willing to partner this freakish thing. Around us, the other women were finding partners among the monstrous creatures, and it was obvious that they expected us to do likewise, for there were females among this ugly race.

"Well, there was no way I was willingly going to lie down

with any of them heathens. And one look at my companions told me they were in agreement."

"It is often too late when we realise the error of our licentious ways," I said, but I do not think he heard me.

He went on, "All of a sudden Ali went berserk. The queer buildings and repulsive statues had already put him ill at ease, but to be confronted with the living reality, and the realisation of what was expected of us – well, it must have been too much. He pulled out his meat cleaver, and with a crazed yell he started laying about with it.

"I drew my cutlass and joined in, hacking and chopping, whilst young Jake swung his fists. It took them by surprise, by God! We were determined to fight our way out of there."

"You mean you attacked them without provocation?" I was astounded. "But that's monstrous."

"Aye! Monstrous! Indeed they were, Father. Such things should not be. They fought back with tooth and claw. And I was near throttled when one of them wrapped his tentacle-arm around my throat."

"Whatever their appearance, they were still part of God's creation," I protested.

"But they were heathen savages."

"They may have been ignorant of God, but surely they should have been given the opportunity of conversion. A good missionary could have brought them the word of the Lord."

But Crawford was not paying attention to me. In his mind, he was back on the island and reliving his experiences.

"I grabbed their leader, and that gave them pause. I had my blade pressed against his scaly skin, and I told my hostage to call off his followers. He croaked out something that caused them to keep their distance. They held back a short while, but soon they came hopping and scrambling after us. I think they were not used to moving about on land, and they certainly found running difficult – so, even with the burden of a hostage, we were able to outpace them.

"We made it to the canoes; Ali pushed one out to sea, whilst Jake holed the others. Jake then took charge of our prisoner, and I cut down the first of the islanders to reach us.

"But I realised that, even though we had rendered the other craft useless, it did not matter. I was sure that the islanders would swim after us. We needed to delay them somehow."

Crawford held his head in his hands. "Poor Jake," he moaned. "He gave up his life so that we might get away."

"How did it happen?" I asked.

Crawford seemed reluctant to speak of it. "It pains me to remember, Father."

"Come now," I chided, "if your companion bravely gave up his life, he at least deserves to have his noble act recounted."

I had expected to hear of the young sailor's heroic sacrifice, but what the sailor said next left me stunned.

"Well, it were a drastic act, but I did the only thing I could think of – I clobbered Jake and left him senseless on the beach, hoping that one of us would appease them."

It was a shocking revelation. One that caused me to swear, "Good God, man!" I was incredulous. "You left your friend at the mercy of enraged savages?"

His next admission was to have me shaking my head in disbelief.

"I would have left Ali behind, too, if I could have, but he was already in the canoe and had seen what I'd done to Jake. Besides, I needed him to row."

"Why, your actions make you more of a savage than these so-called Atlanteans. I pray to God that they showed your friend more mercy than you did!"

Crawford sniffed. "Even if they didn't kill him in revenge there and then, but kept him for their original purpose of mating with one of their women-kind, then I doubt he would have lived much longer."

"What do you mean?"

"It didn't occur to me at the time – the mere thought of those female Atlanteans was bad enough. But I later realised why there were no men on Nia's island."

"I don't follow you, Mr Crawford. What do you mean?" I asked again.

"Well I reckon them females bred like the praying mantis, and after mating they killed their mate."

I said a prayer for poor Jake Webster. Then the seaman continued his tale.

"I could see some of them still meant to pursue us. But there must have been one of them Atlanteans that realised that this was an opportunity for it to seize power for 'imself. For there was a blast on a shell horn, that stopped those that had dived into the sea. A croaked command followed and they returned to the shore.

"My prisoner was furious and began to struggle. Whilst on the shore the Atlanteans picked up poor Jake and returned to their city.

"The canoe was rocking and I feared we would capsize. The priest-king had momentarily got the better of me, when Ali struck him with his meat cleaver."

"It was a lethal blow, no doubt."

"Oh aye, it were lethal all right. Ali had had plenty of experience of using his cleaver, he knew just where to chop; he didn't need to kill the Atlantean."

"I do not condone the taking of another man's life but in doing so he saved yours." I had the unchristian thought that Crawford's was not a life worth saving.

"Well I was mad you can be sure – I had been on the verge of regaining the upper hand. And you see it was my intention to take my prisoner back to civilisation," the sailor grumbled.

"I don't know why I'm surprised by your lack of gratitude, Mr Crawford."

"I could have earned a pretty penny displaying him in a freak show," Crawford complained.

"I couldn't even keep the body – there being no way of preserving it. It corroded quicker than you'd believe possible, and boy what a smell." Crawford's expression was one of disgust.

"You said yourself that the Lascar was unable to cope with the existence of this strange race. Did you really think the three of you could make such a journey together?"

Crawford did not answer, so I tried another question. "How long were you at sea?"

"Days, weeks, months, who knows? I lost track of how long we drifted." Crawford sighed. "Alone, adrift, so long without food or water. Never once coming in sight of land, or a ship of any kind. I thought God had truly forsaken me. I was on the verge of giving up hope; I don't know how much longer I could have survived. And then one day I spotted a ship. Never was I so relieved to see that ship. Rescue at last, thank God."

"Pardon my interruption, but what happened to your companion?" I asked.

"Eh? What?"

"You said you were alone. What happened to Ali?"

"Oh, Ali, yeah, well, Ali." Crawford paused, considering. "Well, I've told you this much, I might as well tell you the rest. You see Ali, he were in a sorry state." Crawford shook his head. "A sorry state, no mistake, well, we both were, if truth be told. There was no way we was both gonna make it like. It was a long time before that ship turned up. And there was no point in us both dying, were there? He weren't gonna make it, and there was no point in me dying of starvation now was there? And there was no way I was ever gonna eat fish ever again, not after what I'd seen on that island."

"What are you saying?" I gasped.

Crawford's sudden grin was maniacal. "You could say,

Father, that for once in his life Ali served up a decent meal. Best food I ever got out of him."

I was aghast. "Mr Crawford, Are you saying what I think you are saying? I despair; you are a truly despicable man. It will take a great deal of thought to decide upon a suitable act of penance for you to perform."

My thoughts raced. I felt sickened by much of what the sailor had admitted to me. But how much truth was there to his wild story? Was he really admitting to murder and cannibalism?

I thought there were inconsistencies to his tale, and I doubted that he had told me the whole truth. Indeed, I half suspected that I was the victim of an old sailor's tall tale.

No doubt he had seen some wild things on his travels. But was Crawford suffering from some sort of madness brought on by the distress of being ship wrecked? It was also evident that he had too strong a liking for rum. Did he suffer from drunken delusions?

And yet he did have that curiously strange crown. How else could he have come by it, I wondered. Piracy perhaps.

Crawford interrupted my thoughts. "You will let me spend the night here, won't you, Father?"

"Well—"

"He fell to his knees again. "I beg of you, Father, give me shelter for the night."

I will admit my first instinct was to again direct him to seek a room at Kirowan's inn. The wretch had admitted to countless dubious and sinful activities, and I was not sure of my own safety if I allowed him to stay.

Perhaps Crawford sensed my feelings for he suddenly became hysterical. "Oh, Lord protect me! The sea wants it back! Verily it is true, here be sea monsters!" he raved.

And then he howled a jumble of harsh guttural gibberish – of which I only recognised one word, the name of the ancient Philistine deity Dagon – before breaking down in tears. "Ah God, forgive this unworthy sinner," he cried.

I chided myself for my doubts. The Lord would protect me. God had obviously directed Patrick Crawford to my door; it was my Christian duty to give shelter to this repentant sinner.

"Very well," I relented, "I can provide you with a bed for the night."

I had expected this to please the old sailor, but he suddenly began to moan. "No, no, no."

"What is wrong?" I asked, confused by his response.

"Please Father; let me spend the night here in your church. Let me spend the night in prayer," he begged. "You did say no one could take me from Lord's house. Let me spend the night here. That way it'll be safer for the both of us."

I was about to ask what he meant by that, when he began to rave again. Most of it sounded like more of the harsh guttural gibberish that he had uttered before. The only part I could make out clearly: "Sanctuary, grant me sanctuary. The Lord have mercy upon me. All life came from the sea, and the sea shall give up its dead. But it will not give me up." And that, I did not entirely understand, although some of it certainly sounded blasphemous.

The poor wretch was obviously disturbed. And so I acquiesced, "Very well, Mr Crawford, you may remain in the church over night." I would get Dr Hodgeson to take a look at him on the morrow.

"Would you like me to stay with you?" I asked.

Crawford smiled, calmer now that I had granted his request. "No, Father, no! The Lord shall protect me."

However, before I left I thought it wise to make sure the church silver and the communion wine was safely locked away. Then I said a final prayer and bid the old sailor, good night, telling him I would return early in the morning.

Upon reaching the door, I looked back. Crawford had again removed the crown from his haversack. He appeared to be gloating over his treasure. He was muttering something – although I doubted whether it was a prayer.

Crawford's prediction of a storm proved correct. That night rain fell in sheets, and the wind howled. The howl of the wind sounded like shrieks of agony and cries of despair.

It was truly terrible, and I shuddered to think how it would be to encounter such a tempest at sea.

Little did I expect that I was soon to learn that there was more to Crawford's story than I had imagined possible.

True to my word, I returned to the church early the next morning.

Inside, ah, you will think me mad. I opened the door, and water lapped out. Seawater, I can still smell the brine. It was not deep now, but it must have been, for everything in the room was awry and wet, and draped with seaweed. And amidst it all, sprawled before the altar was the sailor.

Patrick Crawford was dead, an expression of utmost horror upon his face and seaweed wrapped around his neck; his lungs full of the salt water.

Beside him lay his haversack and the tattered remnants of a yellow cloth, but the strange crown had gone.

The sudden disappearance of Father Michael O'Donnell caused great shock and consternation among his congregation.

The strange story revealed in the above document, may have some bearing on the matter.

Written in his own hand, it was found in the priest's house, and perhaps serves to illustrate the state of his mind prior to his disappearance.

Although Donald Kirowan remembers a man fitting the description of Patrick Crawford drinking in his bar, the man never asked about lodging for the night.

Certainly Father O'Donnell never contacted me about Patrick Crawford. And no trace of the sailor's body has been found. Although, curiously the church did have a slight smell reminiscent of the sea, for a few days after Father O'Donnell's disappearance.

Two weeks later, Father Michael's body was found, washed up on a beach some forty miles from his home.

A pair of reliable witness testified that they had seen someone matching the priest's description on the cliffs a few miles further up the coast.

But whether Father O'Donnell fell from the cliffs by accident, or by the intervention of another's hand, or – heaven forefend – by his own choice, is unlikely to ever be known.

Dr Thomas Hodgeson, Physician.

DEATH ON THE LINE

Hugh Clifford glanced at the station clock, and sighed loudly. He was one of six people waiting on the single platform of Barrow Ashton railway station for the eight thirty a.m. train into Mortbury. The clock now read eight fifty-five.

The others standing on Platform 1 were a youth whose features were obscured by his hood and a cloud of cigarette smoke, a young woman with two small children – one of each sex. Clifford made a mental note to sit well away from those four. And a smartly dressed older man, who was cleaning his glasses. Clifford paced around in frustration, made a cursory examination of the timetable again – he knew it off by heart – then paced around some more. Again he sighed, although this time in relief, for he could hear in the distance the approaching train.

After the train had come to a halt, the doors opened, and no one got off. The waiting commuters moved to board the train. The teenager barging past the others, jostling the elderly gentleman in the process.

"Out of my way, granddad!"

The man staggered, but recovered from the shove that Jason Marshman had given him.

"Fuckin' nonce!" Jason muttered, tossing his cigarette butt away.

"Are you all right?" Clifford enquired.

"What? Oh, yes. Thank you." The man smiled.

The smile quickly faded, and he glared at the yob's back. "I've got your number, sonny," he said softly.

Politely, Clifford waited for the others to board the train before getting on himself.

The reason for Clifford's journey was simple. This was a shopping trip; normally he enjoyed such excursions, as he would usually spend his time browsing in book- and record shops. But this was a shopping spree he was not looking forward to. His purpose to buy a mobile phone. He was a self-styled Luddite, and up until now he had avoided owning one. But after considerable badgering from his friends, and some work acquaintances, he had acquiesced and finally agreed to purchase one. Although that was more to do with the fact that he was fed up of the constant pestering to get one, and the looks he would receive when it was revealed that he did not possess such a device, than any real desire to own one.

He was meeting up with one of these friends – Jeremy Sheridan had at least had the decency to offer to help Clifford find the right phone.

As the train set off, Clifford found a seat. He took out his book and began to read. After a few moments he was roused from his reading by the guard.

Previous experience had taught him it was a waste of time enquiring why the train had been delayed, but he couldn't resist commenting as he bought his ticket. "Running late again."

"That's right, sir. Very observant of you." The guard smiled insincerely. "Not to worry though, sir. We'll be able to go faster on this next stretch and regain some time."

"Glad to hear it."

Clifford had not long resumed reading when a phone rang.

"Yeah, I'm on the train," the recipient of the call – a fat, bearded man – said loudly. Clifford tried to shut out the noisy one-sided conversation that followed – the fat man often having to repeat himself.

The yobbish youth had met up with a group of his friends; they were all drinking cans of lager and getting rather rowdy. Unable to concentrate on his reading, Clifford noticed that the man he had spoken to on the platform was also engaged in making a phone call.

The elderly man finished his call, and consulted a notepad

that evidently bore a list of telephone numbers. He crossed off the number he had dialled, and then rang the next one on his list. His call lasted long enough for him to say just four words. Then he repeated the process, over and over again.

Despite himself, Clifford watched, strangely fascinated. The man was too far away to hear and unlike most mobile phone users on board trains, the softly spoken old man did not raise his voice. Clifford wondered briefly whether the old man was mentally unwell and was calling people just to say – *I'm on the train*. That was four words after all, and it seemed to be what every telephone caller on every train, he had the misfortune to overhear seemed to say at some point in their phone conversation. Sometimes more than once if the reception was poor.

Somewhere on the one carriage train a small child began to wail, Clifford frowned unable to ascertain whether it were male or female. Not that it mattered; the sound was annoying whatever its source.

The dapperly dressed old man checked his watch and smiled at Clifford. Embarrassed that the man had noticed his observation, Clifford quickly returned his gaze to his book.

The old man appeared unconcerned that Clifford had been watching him, and for the rest of the journey continued making his calls whilst Clifford – who had abandoned any attempt to read due to the increasing noise that his fellow passengers were making – concentrated on the passing countryside.

"Ah, Hugh! There you are." Jeremy Sheridan greeted his friend with a roguish smile. "I was beginning to think you'd changed your mind."

"Sorry, Jeremy. Although, I don't know as it should be me apologising. Bloody train was running late!"

"Well, if you had a car you wouldn't have to use them."

Clifford held up a hand in protest. "Don't start, Jeremy. Be satisfied with your victory."

Sheridan laughed. "Ah, Hugh, we'll soon have you living in the twenty-first century – even if we have to drag you kicking and screaming."

"No, Jeremy," Clifford protested, "I vow I shall succumb no further."

"Come on then, you old Luddite." Sheridan led the way out of the railway station. Laughing, he said, "If we get a move on, we'll have time to have a look for a computer for you."

Clifford shuddered. "Dear Lord," he muttered. "Where will it end?"

Jason Marshman drained another can of lager and tossed it out of the window of the Ford Fiesta.

"Can't this thing go any faster?" Scott leaned forward in the passenger seat to turn up the volume of the car stereo.

Jason pressed his foot down on the accelerator. To the accompaniment of the latest hip-hop CD, he drove precariously and well past the speed limit. He glanced in the rear-view mirror. "Hey, Bazza, stop hogging the joint, man."

"Yeah, yeah," Bazza said from the backseat.

Beside him, Deano whined, "It's my turn next."

Scott opened another can of beer. "Bloody heap of junk. Why'd we have to nick this one?"

"Shut up, Scott. What's the matter with you?"

"Nothin'."

Deano was busy updating his Facebook status on his mobile. "He's pissed off that Julie Tate hasn't called him."

Jason laughed. "She's a slag."

"That's why he's pissed off she hasn't called."

"Shut up!"

"Ring her then," Jason urged his friend.

"No way!"

"Why not?"

"She's a slag!"

Jason laughed again. He would have been unaware of his phone ringing if he had not had it set on vibrate.

"Maybe this is her calling me." Pulling the phone from his pocket, Jason thumbed the answer button. "Yeah?"

A soft voice spoke four words.

"You what … the fuck?" Jason suddenly lost control of the stolen car.

"What the fuck are you doing, Jase?" Deano shouted.

"I can't control it!"

"Stop fucking around!" Scott yelled.

The vehicle veered from one side of the road to the other. He struggled with the steering wheel, but whichever way he turned it it would not direct the car from its course.

"Slow down, man!"

"Hold on!" Frantically, Jason slammed on the brakes, but the Fiesta would not slow.

"Oh Jesus!"

"Stop the fucking car!"

"I can't!"

"You fuckin' maniac, Jase." Bazza laughed.

Three phones rang simultaneously. Deano still had his gripped in his hand, he had been about to call 999. He read aloud the text message that had been sent to all three passengers – *My name is Death.*

"You what?"

"Is this some kind of sick joke?"

Jason decided he had to get out of the car. He was not wearing a seat belt and he opened the door.

"What are you doing?" Scott reached for the steering wheel. "Don't be fucking stupid!"

Jason wasn't listening and threw himself from the speeding

vehicle.

"Fuck!"

"Oh God!"

Straight into the path of a lorry that was coming in the opposite direction. Jason didn't even have time to scream before the lorry hit him. The young joyrider was killed instantly.

His friends did scream as the Fiesta went off the road straight into a brick wall. Bazza was the only one who survived until the car's fuel tank exploded.

After a shopping trip that had seen Hugh Clifford make not one but two concessions to the modern age the two friends had gone to Jeremy Sheridan's apartment. Although Sheridan had tried to convince him to buy an I-pod, Clifford had purchased a portable compact disc player. From now on, his train journeys would no longer be blighted by the menace of other people's mobile phone conversations and crying children, he would be cocooned in a world of classical music.

"Now that wasn't so bad, was it, Hugh?" said Sheridan, pouring his friend a drink.

"What a rigmarole," complained Clifford. "So many to choose from, and then the range of payment plans! All of them expensive of course. Ah! What a dreadful experience. And not one I plan to repeat anytime soon - and to think there are those people who regularly change their make and model of phone."

"You've got to stay up to date." Sheridan smiled.

"But why? When something works perfectly adequately? Why change it?"

"Technology marches on, Hugh."

"Cameras, Bluetooth, whatever that is, apps." Clifford threw up his hands. "It's all so confusing."

"You'll soon be wondering how you ever managed without it all."

"Oh no, I won't." Clifford reached for his glass. "I will only make calls myself in emergencies. I will not become addicted to it like so many people have. Everywhere you go you see them - phone permanently attached to the side of their head, or slavishly typing their text messages. Like a lot of zombies!"

Sheridan laughed.

"There was an example of one such addict on the train this morning. Perhaps addict is not the right word to use, but it will do."

"Oh?"

"He was armed with phone, notepad and pen. Written on his pad was obviously a list of phone numbers. He would dial a number, wait for a response, say something briefly, and hang up. Then, with a satisfied smile upon his face, he would cross out the number."

"How odd."

"Yes," agreed Clifford. "Phone call after phone call he made, only uttering what could be the selfsame message."

"What do you think he was saying?"

"I don't know." Clifford shrugged. "I did wonder whether it was: I'm on the train."

Sheridan grinned.

"Gave me the creeps actually." Clifford finished his brandy.

"Another drink, Hugh?"

"Hmm, yes please, Jeremy. Funny thing is he was waiting at the station before me, but I'd certainly never seen him in Barrow Ashton before."

"Really? What did he look like?" Sheridan asked, refilling their glasses.

"Why? What difference does it make?"

Sheridan shrugged. "Just curious."

"Well, he was somewhat upon the short side, slim, elderly – certainly at least twenty years older than either of us. Very smartly dressed in a dark, not quite black suit, that looked quite expensive. He wore glasses and a somewhat ostentatious bow tie. His grey hair was almost white."

"Very—" Sheridan began to say, but he was interrupted.

"Ye Gods!" Clifford cried, as his new mobile phone began to ring. "It's started already."

"That's odd." Sheridan frowned. "You've not had chance to tell anyone your new number yet."

"Exactly, I thought by getting this damn thing that I would at least escape the plague of the call centre."

"Well answer it, man," Sheridan urged.

Clifford pressed a button, and held the phone to his ear. "Hello, Hugh Clifford speaking. Who's calling?"

Clifford recognised the softly spoken voice that said, "My name is Death."

He paled, and held the phone out to his friend. "It's for you."

"Oh?" Puzzled, Sheridan took the proffered phone, and turned away, to stand looking out of the window. He had a picturesque view of the park. There was a man with whitish-grey-coloured hair sitting on a bench. He appeared to be crossing out something written on a notepad.

"Hello?" Sheridan said. There was a thump behind him. "Do be quiet, Hugh, I can't hear. Hello? Who is this? Is there anybody there?"

There was no response.

"That's odd, there's no one there. They must have hung up." Sheridan moved away from the window. "Do you recognise the num …? Oh." Clifford was nowhere to be seen. "Hugh? Where the devil are you?" Sheridan took another step forward and gasped, "Hugh!" when he saw he had fallen to the floor.

Dialling 999, Jeremy Sheridan knelt by his friend desperately trying to find a pulse, but the line was dead, and so was Hugh Clifford.

THE NECRONOMICON

At first I did not recognise the man on my doorstep, and had half a mind to pretend to be out. Yet, when he glanced briefly upwards, there was something about his face that stirred my memory. Not so much the features, but rather the man's superior expression, that seemed somehow familiar.

He was a little under six feet in height, and had thinning, sandy-coloured hair. He was carrying a brown leather briefcase.

As I observed the caller surreptitiously from the upstairs window, I saw him look at his watch impatiently. And although I anticipated he would only turn out to be a door-to-door salesman or similar, I hurried downstairs to open the door and see what the fellow wanted.

Before I could speak, he boomed out a greeting, "Hello Durward."

At once I recognised the distinctive, deep, Welsh voice. "My Goodness, Rhys-Morgan!" I said in amazement.

"Yes it is." The Welshman granted me the briefest of smiles.

We shook hands. "Well, this is a surprise." It had been many years since I had last seen, or even spoken with Gwyn Rhys-Morgan.

I stepped aside to allow him into the house.

"I hope you don't mind me turning up like this, all unannounced."

"Not at all," I replied. "Come on in."

"In here, is it?" Rhys-Morgan ignored the door to the sitting room, choosing instead to enter my library.

I followed him in. "Unerring as usual, Gwyn."

"Could hardly miss the smell, Durward."

"Ah, of course. Well, make yourself comfortable. Can I take your coat and briefcase?"

But Rhys-Morgan paid me no heed, instead putting his case in one of the pair of armchairs and slinging his coat over the back of the seat. Quickly he crossed the room and began studying the books that filled my bookcases. That came as no surprise.

I was about to ask what he would have to drink, but my guest pre-empted me. "I'll have a whisky please, Durward."

"It must be nearly fifteen years," I said, handing him a glass. And I still found it annoying how he would call me 'Durward' after the Walter Scott novel rather than use my name – Quentin.

"Yes, it must." Rhys-Morgan paused in his examination of my shelves to take a generous sample of his drink. "This is good." He drained the glass. "I'll have another."

We had been at Cambridge together. Although we weren't exactly good friends, it was through our shared interest in rare books that we knew each other. It was evident he hadn't changed his manner.

I poured him another whisky, and a silence ensued as Rhys-Morgan scanned the titles that lined the walls. I was about to comment on how I had obtained a particular volume, but he held up a hand to stop me.

Awkwardly, I waited until he had finished his silent perusal.

"An impressive collection," he said at last, taking the seat that was unoccupied by his coat and case.

"Thank you." I remained standing.

"I suppose you're wondering what's brought me to your door after all this time." Once again he had pre-empted my question.

"Well, yes, I was actually."

"I have it."

"It?" I queried.

"It." Rhys-Morgan nodded.

I was puzzled. "I don't understand, Gwyn."

What he said next astounded me.

"*The Necronomicon*," he stated simply.

I gasped audibly. "*The Necronomicon*?"

The Necronomicon: The book of the mad Arab, Abdul Alhazred. A legendary book of blasphemous and cosmic revelations. That utmost grail for seekers of occult knowledge, and of many bibliophiles. And Rhys-Morgan's taste had always leaned towards the outré.

"Yes."

"But how? Where did you find it?"

"My search was long, and often frustrating, but I always remained persistent. I began with libraries and museums, antiquarian bookshops, eventually widening my search.

"Would you believe the British Museum had the audacity to deny me access to their rare books collection? Perhaps they had some inkling of my intention to make their copy my own." Rhys-Morgan paused, apparently brooding.

"It was the same story again and again, at the Bibliotheque Nationale in Paris, and in Rome, and Cairo. Miskatonic University in America, as well. Have you ever been to America, Durward?"

I shook my head.

"Terrible place. You'd do well to avoid it." Rhys-Morgan frowned. "In so many places, I was either refused permission to view the book, or my enquiries met with denials that the book even existed."

I found what Rhys-Morgan said next to be somewhat far-fetched.

"I have travelled the world, not just in body, but in astral form. My quest has taken me to many strange places and I have witnessed even stranger things."

"How extraordinary."

"You think I'm being fanciful don't you, Durward?"

"Well, I'm not sure I follow you exactly, Gwyn."

"It's all right." He waved a hand dismissively. "How could you know? You have spent your life blissfully ignorant of the true nature of the world around us."

I didn't know what to say to that, so I said nothing.

"From major cities of the world to rundown and decrepit

towns in rural New England. I have infiltrated cults of diabolic purpose, and searched the tombs of necromancers that lie in ghoul-haunted graveyards."

Fanciful was the word all right.

"But all this was without success. Yet I did not give up. Then after hunting high and low, and far and wide, I finally tracked down a copy. Would you believe that after all my travels, I located one in an obscure part of Gloucestershire, of all places?"

"However did you afford it? You must have come into a great deal of money, or had one of those incredible pieces of luck where you found it going for a song."

"It was in the possession of a man called James Goodman. I managed to make him part with it."

"Congratulations, Gwyn. I must say I'm honoured that you should think to inform me after all this time."

I refilled our glasses, and asked, "But have you read it?" At the same time eager that he had, but also afraid that he might have done so. For *The Necronomicon* has a dark reputation. It is said that its contents can drive a man insane.

"Oh yes, I have read it. My mind reeled at the cosmic revelations, the unholy and unimaginable truths it contains. Yes, I have drunk deep of its forbidden knowledge."

Despite what Rhys-Morgan said, I wanted to see it for myself. I eyed his briefcase. "And you have it with you now." A statement rather than a question.

He nodded.

"May I see it?"

"Of course." He rose, took his case from the other chair and moved to my desk. I joined him, and he opened it and took out the fabled *Necronomicon*.

It was a large volume – a folio, I estimated at least a thousand pages in length, and bound in dark black leather.

"Incredible."

With a trembling hand I caressed the cover, then carefully

opened the book. "My God, Gwyn! This becomes even more incredible. I had anticipated John Dee's translation – but this is remarkable."

Rhys-Morgan had managed to obtain the Italian printing of 1501, printed in black letter gothic type.

"Yes," he replied, "I too thought that there were no longer any copies of this edition extant. However, I suspect that it is not the original binding."

I marvelled at the pages of text – the fantastic legends that were the ravings of a man thought insane.

Here and there were marginal notes written by numerous different hands. There were stains that might well have been blood. Some pages were torn and a few entirely missing – not surprising considering the book's great age.

I puzzled over strange cosmological diagrams. Wondered at perplexing rituals of sorcery and a blasphemous religion. And shuddered at illustrations of monstrous creatures labelled: *From Life*.

"Wonderful!" I declared. My thoughts were covetous. "How much do you want for it?"

"Oh, it's not for sale."

I sighed. It was the answer I'd expected.

"I doubt whether you'd be prepared to pay the price anyway," he said, cryptically.

Then after a moment he said, "At the back of the book you will find there is a list of names, such as is sometimes found in a family bible."

I turned towards the rear of the book and found the list.

The first name was Anotonio Carlucci with a set of dates 1501-1505. Gian Mollisimo 1505-1519 was next. Then Ricardo Del Vascao, 1519; followed by Fernando Diaz 1519-1535. After him was John Maltravers, 1535-1554.

"It's impossible that these are dates of birth and death," I said. "They must be dates of ownership of the book."

Another thought occurred to me, "These names, they appear to be written all in the same hand."

Rhys-Morgan nodded.

"For someone to have traced the ownership of the book back through its history is a remarkable act of scholarship. But you are not responsible?"

Rhys-Morgan shook his head. "No."

I read further down the list. Raschid Ibn Malik caught my eye. His dates read 1609-1759. "But that's impossible, a hundred and fifty years."

Rhys-Morgan smiled at my bewildered expression.

"Imagine how I impatiently turned the pages to find the end of the list, eager to add my name and thus confirm my rightful ownership.

"Then imagine how my mind reeled when I saw beneath the name of James Goodman, already written in that same red ink, my own name."

"What? But that's impossible."

"Is it?"

I turned to the end of the list. Sure enough below James Goodman 1934-1936, was Gwyn Rhys-Morgan 1936-.

"Well then perhaps Goodman, knowing he was going to sell the book to you, had already appended your name to the list"

"That's just it. You see, Durward; Goodman wouldn't sell. No matter how much I offered him he refused."

"Then how?"

"I killed him."

"You did what?" I don't know which stunned me more: the fact that Rhys-Morgan had killed a man, or the casual way that he had admitted it.

"You do see that I had to? Don't you, Durward? I had to have it, it was rightfully mine."

I smiled and nodded, thinking it wise not to antagonise him.

Rhys-Morgan continued, "You said that the dates were dates

of ownership rather than dates of birth and death. You were partly right. Ownership yes, but also year of death."

I frowned. "Are you sure?"

"I did do some research of my own, and found out about some of the names on the list."

"And?"

Rhys-Morgan began picking out names from the list. "Ricardo Del Vascao, tortured to death by the Inquisition in 1519. Agnes Lamprey was burnt at the stake in 1603. In 1759 Raschid Ibn Malik was stoned. In 1793 Louis Rocheteau was—"

I interrupted, "Let me guess, another victim of the Reign of Terror?"

"Perhaps. It's not clear what happened exactly. Although what is certain is that he was torn to pieces, various parts of his body were found all over Paris."

Rhys-Morgan continued his morbid recitation, "Matthew Horne was killed in the Indian Mutiny of 1857—"

"Well, lots of people were killed during the Indian Mutiny," I pointed out.

"Yes, but Horne's body was found covered in curious bite marks and completely drained of blood." Rhys-Morgan smiled. "Josiah Wellsby had it after him – he committed suicide in 1859. Every one of them died in the latter year listed."

"What about Goodman? How did he come to have the book?" I consulted the list; the name above Goodman's was Victor Goodman.

"His father," Rhys-Morgan said. "He inherited it from his father."

"There you are then, he died in bed, after living to a ripe old age," I said, with an optimism I did not really feel.

"Actually, you are almost correct, Goodman senior did die in bed. James Goodman boasted that he smothered his father with a pillow. His father got it during the war, looted it off a German he killed." Rhys-Morgan pointed to the name above Victor

Goodman's: Pieter Mueller.

Suddenly Rhys-Morgan began to laugh wildly. "Don't you get it yet, Durward?"

"Calm down, Gwyn," I urged. "What ever do you mean?"

"What does the title *Necronomicon* actually mean?" he asked.

"The title's in Greek," I said. "It's the name given to the book by its translator, Theodorus Philetas. "Mentally I translated the title. "It means … My God!"

"Yes, Durward, imagine how I felt reading my name in *The Book of Dead Names*."

It was not long after his visit that the police arrested Rhys-Morgan following an anonymous tip-off.

He was found guilty of James Goodman's murder. And when the death penalty was carried out, the year marking his demise, and the end of his period of ownership of *The Necronomicon*, appeared written by that unknown hand, in that same red ink.

And the name of the book's new owner duly appeared beneath his.

Rhys-Morgan was wrong; I am prepared to pay the price – eventually.

You see, I believe that somewhere in its pages Raschid Ibn Malik found the secret of a preternaturally long life, and I shall find it too.

Quentin Richley,
April 1938.

Addendum: Quentin Richley died in August 1940, one of the many casualties of the Second World War.

A BIT TASTY

"Let me get this straight—you want *me*, to make *you*, more attractive to women?"

Kevin was surprised at how beautiful the witch was. She wore a little black dress that showed off her shapely figure. He'd been unable to take his eyes off her rear as she'd led him into the open-plan kitchen. Her long hair was blonde, eyes blue, and he'd never seen a witch with such a cute little nose before.

And those lips ...

Kevin's thoughts began to wander.

The witch clicked her fingers. "Is something the matter?" she asked.

"What?" Kevin spluttered. "I'm sorry ... I was wondering what it would be like to feel your mouth on ..."

"Watch it!" warned the witch.

Kevin blushed and apologised again. "I didn't expect you to be so beautiful," he admitted.

"Oh? And what were you expecting?"

Kevin stammered, but before he could say anything, the witch spoke again, "Did you think I'd be an ancient hag with a large hooked nose?"

"Well, um ..."

"You've been reading too many fairy stories."

"I'm sorry," Kevin apologised for a third time.

"Aye well, for all you know, maybe I really am an old crone, and I used my magic to make *myself* beautiful." She laughed. "You wouldn't have much confidence in my ability to help you if I did have a big nose and warts, would you now?"

"No, I guess not. And the answer is yes."

"Yes, what?"

"The answer to your question – yes, I want to be more attractive to women. Can you help me?"

The witch looked him up and down.

"I'm desperate," he said. "I've tried everything else."

The witch didn't doubt his claim. Kevin was a lanky young man with less than plain features, which were not helped by his spots. His clothes were unfashionable and ill-fitting. And his tangle of ginger hair could do with a good combing.

"Your advert said you did 'Love philtres, glamorous enchantments, spells to induce desire ...'"

"Yes, I can do all of those things, and much more," she boasted.

"Well, they all sound good to me."

"Is there someone in particular you wish to fall in love with you? Or do you want to drive all women wild with desire?" the witch asked.

"No, no, not at all. I can imagine that leading to all sorts of trouble."

"Good, because I would refuse to do such a thing."

"But, you can help me?"

Despite the witch's earlier boast, it would not be easy. She sighed. "Very well."

"Great!"

"It won't come cheap though."

"How much?"

"One hundred and fifty pounds."

"One—" Kevin began.

The witch interrupted. "I don't haggle!"

"Fine."

"Payment first."

"Very well. Will you take a cheque?"

The witch shook her head. "Cash."

Kevin took out his wallet, and counted out the money.

The witch went to a shelf of books. Kevin could see that they were cookery books, apart from one that stood out from the rest, which the witch selected. It was a large volume, covered in black leather and bound with brass hinges.

"Sit down," she invited, as she studied her spellbook. "Make yourself comfortable. This may take a while."

After a few minutes of study she announced, "Found it. This should do the trick." And to herself, she mumbled, "If anything can."

Kevin started to rise from the sofa.

"No, no, you stay there," the witch instructed.

She found a large saucepan, then opened a cupboard and began selecting an assortment of jars and bottles. She arranged these on her worktop.

From where he was sitting, Kevin could see that some of them appeared to contain herbs. But others he was not so sure about. Perhaps he was better off not knowing, he decided, remembering something about witches and their penchant for eye of newt and tongue of toad.

The witch began mixing the ingredients in the saucepan, which she heated on the Aga. As she did so, she read from the book in an impressively stentorian voice.

Despite this, Kevin could not make out the words she spoke.

Eventually, the witch proffered a tall glass of bubbling greenish liquid. "Here you are then."

Reluctantly, Kevin accepted it. "It stinks."

"And then some," the witch agreed.

"I suppose I have to drink it."

"Well, you could rub it over your body, but I wouldn't recommend it. It'd have a totally different effect than the one you're after."

Kevin lifted the glass to his lips, and took a sip. "Aaargh! It's disgusting."

"Aye, well the best medicines usually are. Now drink it down quick or it won't work."

"Oh well, here goes." Kevin drained the glass, his expression one of disgust.

"Well? How do you feel?" the witch asked.

"Apart from nauseous you mean?"

The witch nodded.

"Disappointed." Kevin sighed. "There's nothing happening. I don't feel any different." He got up from the sofa.

"Do I look any different?" he asked, studying his reflection in the full-length mirror.

Ruefully, the witch shook her head. "I'm afraid not."

"No, I can't see any difference, either." Kevin sighed again. "I should have known that not even magic could help me." He turned back to the witch. "Do I get a refund?" he wondered aloud.

"Hold your horses! These things can take time."

"Hey!" Kevin yelled suddenly.

"What is it? Are you all right?"

"Tingling. There's this tingling sensation in my toes," he explained. "Is that supposed to happen?"

The witch nodded, although truthfully she did not know. This was a piece of magic she had never attempted before.

"It's spreading. Up my legs."

"Does it hurt?"

"No ... No, it feels great." Kevin glanced in the mirror. "I don't see any physical change."

"Maybe it takes more time."

"Yeah, maybe. Or maybe it just instils a sense of confidence. Women are supposed to like men who are confident, aren't they?" The witch wasn't sure whether that was a statement or a question, but before she could reply Kevin asked, "What does it say in your book?"

"I'll have a look."

However, before she could consult her spellbook, Kevin gave a cry. "Wow! My whole body is tingling. I feel great. I feel as if I could go out and get any woman I wanted."

The witch was not so sure, but she kept quiet.

Kevin began to shake. "Whoooooaaa!" he yelled, then was

110

suddenly silent.

An amazing transformation had taken place.

"Well, I never. I never expected that." The witch moved closer to Kevin.

"Hmm, very tasty, very tasty indeed. I fancy a piece of that myself," she murmured.

And she wouldn't have been the only one. The witch licked her lips appreciatively, her hand reaching for the new-look Kevin.

Kevin, who had suddenly been transformed into a rather large bar of chocolate.

A FISTFUL OF VENGEANCE

The man known as Crazy Cal Harper listened at the door of the hotel room. Not that anyone used that epithet in Harper's presence – not unless they were crazy themselves. Anyone who did was likely to end up dead.

Harper smiled, this was the right room – there was no mistaking the voice of the man inside. Brett Franklin's drawl was quite distinctive. Harper straightened and took a step back. The smile had gone from his face. He took a deep breath, and then kicked the door open.

There was a shriek as the door slammed against the wall. The tableaux that was unveiled brought the smile back to Harper's face.

On the bed lay a naked saloon girl. Standing beside the bed was a red-faced Brett Franklin. Harper had caught him in the act of undressing, and his britches were around his ankles.

"What the hell?" Franklin had yelled at the sudden interruption.

Harper stepped into the hotel room. "Hello Franklin," he said. "You forgot to put the *do not disturb* sign on the door."

"Uh!" Franklin grunted. "It's you!"

"Surprised to see me?"

Franklin glanced at his gun belt. The gun belt that he had unbuckled in such a rush, and draped over the back of a chair. Trying to reach it would mean certain death.

Instead, he said, "It's been a long time."

Harper nodded. "Too long."

"When did you get out?"

"Not soon enough." Harper pushed the door shut behind him.

Franklin frowned. "You've come for your share of the money?"

"Kinda perceptive of you. Now, why don't you sit down on

the bed and tell me where it is?"

"Why not?" Franklin shrugged and sat down.

"Well, where is it?"

"I'll take you to it."

"I've grown kinda particular about the company I keep. I'll go alone. Now, where is it?"

"Don't worry, Cal, it's safe."

"So where did you put it."

"I buried it."

"You did what?"

"I buried it, what did you expect me to do, put it in a bank?"

"All right, just where did you bury it?"

"If I tell you that, you'll shoot me."

Harper laughed. "What makes you think I won't shoot you anyway?"

"Yeah, that had kinda crossed my mind, Cal." Franklin said, trying to calculate his chances of getting out of this hotel room alive.

"I'm getting kinda tired of this, Franklin. Where did you bury the money?"

"In a cemetery."

"In a cemetery," repeated Harper. He laughed again. "Well, I guess that makes sense. Which one?"

"I'll show you, Cal, I'll take you to it."

"God dammit, Franklin!" Harper shouted. "You'll tell me which cemetery, and in which grave. And you'll tell me right now!"

"But if I tell you, you'll kill me," Franklin protested.

"There's worse things than dying, care to find out what, Brett?"

"No."

Harper sighed, and his tone grew conciliatory. "Look, I haven't come here to kill you, Brett. In fact, I'm offended you could think such a thing of me. And if it'll make it any easier for

114

you, I swear on my mother's life that I won't kill you. How's that?"

"You swear?"

"Sure, I swear. Hell, Brett, what do you take me for? Sure I'm a bank robber, an' I've killed plenty of folk in my time, but I ain't some kinda low-down, mean, murdering bastard, am I?"

That was a question that Franklin was well aware of the answer to; however, he chose not to answer it.

"Hell, I ain't even drawn my gun, yet." Harper sounded offended. "I think I could be forgiven for thinking that you were aiming on keeping all that gold for yourself. That's not the case now, is it?"

Franklin sighed. "All right. It's in the Ridge Hill cemetery. That big Civil War one."

"That is a big one," Harper agreed. His tone hardened again. "Which grave?"

Franklin licked his lips, then nodded. "Very well. The money is buried in the grave of one Al Gibson."

"Al Gibson, hey?" Harper smiled.

"Yeah, Al Gibson."

Harper's hand went to his pistol. "It may surprise you to know, Brett, that this pains me, but I have to do it."

"Hey, come on, Cal. I kept the money safe. I've told you where it is. You don't have to do this."

Harper smiled. "Tell you what; I'll give you a chance."

"Look, Cal, You can have all the money, my share, all of it."

"My you have grown perceptive." Harper's expression grew stern. "Pull your pants up, Franklin."

Warily, Franklin did so, half expecting to die in the process. He wondered whether he could make an escape by jumping from the window.

Harper seemed to read his thoughts. He glanced at the girl who cowered on the bed. She was pretty, blonde-haired, firm-breasted. "What's your name?"

115

"Glad," she answered. "It's short for Gladys."

"Pretty name for a pretty lady," opined Harper.

Glad smiled at the complement.

"Well now, Glad, you move over there, by the window, that way you're outta harm's way. Wouldn't want to see you get hurt now, would we?"

"But," Glad protested, "everybody will be able to see me naked."

Harper grinned, amused by the whore's sudden concern for her modesty. "Just do it, darlin'."

Pouting, Glad got off the bed, wrapped a sheet around herself, and went to stand in front of the window, blocking Franklin's possible route of escape.

Franklin cursed silently.

"Say something, Brett?" Harper asked.

"No." Franklin shook his head.

Harper nodded. "Good. Now, go put on your gun belt."

Briefly, Franklin had thought about launching himself at Harper but had dismissed the idea. Even while he had been distracted by the whore, Harper would have drawn and filled him with lead before he got anywhere near him. His only chance – slim though it was – was in a gunfight, and he began to cross the room.

Harper waited until Franklin had almost reached the chair, before pulling his gun and opening fire.

Glad screamed.

The shot sent Franklin crashing against the wall. "You bastard!" He yelled in pain and anger. "Thought you were gonna give me a chance?" Franklin slid down the wall, hands pressed against where the bullet had entered his body.

"What can I say? 'Cept I lied."

"Why? I told you where it is …" Franklin was crying. His hands could not prevent the blood that wept from his chest. "That you could have it all."

"Sure, you did," Harper agreed. "And one day, you'd come after me. Gunning to kill me."

"I'll come after you … you … you bastard," swore the dying Franklin.

Harper shook his head. "You should save your breath."

"I'll kill you! I swear it." Somehow, Franklin managed to draw enough strength to utter his oath. "You hear me, Harper? I'll have my vengeance. I'll kill you!"

"You know, it's surprising how quickly you can grow tired of someone's voice." Harper calmly took aim, fired, and Brett Franklin slumped over, dead.

Harper laughed. "Guess there were limits on his powers of perception after all."

He turned his attention to Glad. She was trembling in the corner of the room.

"He paid you?"

The girl nodded, too frightened to speak.

Harper smiled. "Well, in that case …" He grabbed the whore by the wrist. "What's paid for is paid for … And with my money, after all." Harper thrust the girl onto the bed and began to unbutton his trousers.

Harper crested the top of Ridge Hill, and whistled in response to what lay before him. Below was row after row of graves marked by wooden crosses. Even though he knew whose grave he was looking for, it would still take a long time to find. Hell, there could even be more than one Al Gibson buried here.

Harper tethered his horse to a cross, unburdened it of the tools he had brought with him, and began his search.

Harper paused to drink from his canteen. He kicked a stone in frustration. "Where the hell are you, Al Gibson?" he suddenly shouted. Eerily his voice echoed, repeating his question.

Harper laughed. Hell was probably where Gibson was.

Farther along the row, a crow alighted upon one of the crosses. "Get," Harper shouted, throwing a stone at the bird. The black bird took off, and Harper resumed his search.

Moments later Harper gave a whoop. "Well, I'll be damned." Remarkably, the wooden marker where the crow had landed was the grave of Al Gibson – died February 1862. With renewed enthusiasm, Harper began to dig.

The coffin uncovered, Harper threw aside the spade. It had not been buried deep. Harper grinned, at last the gold would be his.

Gathering some rope, he attached it to the coffin. Harper took a deep breath, then began to haul the oblong box from the hole in the ground.

Breathing heavily from the effort, Harper found his crowbar. "Soon have you free."

Levering with the crowbar, the lid came off easily. To reveal a skeleton, the remnants of its uniform so faded as to be indiscernible as to which side Gibson had fought for in the war. There was no money.

"You bastard, Franklin!" Harper yelled. Angrily he reached into the coffin and yanked free Gibson's skull. "You dirty cheatin' bastard!" Harper threw the skull aside. He began to beat the ground with his fist, ranting and raving.

Abruptly a shadow fell across Harper. Eyes narrowing, he looked up.

"Taken to grave robbery, have we, Harper?" The man who spoke was tall and lean, and his gun was pointed at the outlaw.

"You're the only jackal around these parts, bounty killer."

The bounty hunter rolled his cheroot from one side of his mouth to the other. "I can take you in dead or alive, Harper."

Harper sneered. "You think so?" he said, getting to his feet.

"Choice is yours. Now either go for your gun, or take off that belt."

Harper scowled. "All right, all right. I ain't gonna let you kill me now, am I?"

"Take off that belt then. Slowly now." The bounty hunter pointed. "Now, throw it over there, and then put your hands up in the air."

Harper unbuckled his belt, but instead of pitching it where instructed, he suddenly tossed it at the bounty hunter's face.

The gunman flinched aside, firing as he did so, but Harper had already hurled himself out of the way. Again the gunman fired, just missing the rolling Harper. Bowie knife in hand Harper rose. Recklessly he charged the bounty hunter.

Gun blazing, the gunman could not understand how he had not hit his prey. Then Harper grimaced, as a bullet grazed his head. Blood ran down his cheek, and his charge slowed to a stagger. Abruptly he fell backwards.

"Seems like I've got you now, Harper." The bounty hunter approached warily, reloading his pistol as he did so.

"Do you want me to put a bullet in you, just to make sure that you're dead?" The bounty hunter kept his gun trained on the murderer.

Harper groaned, his hand clawing desperately for his dropped knife. It lay just out of his reach.

"My, my, that is a vicious looking blade. Wouldn't do for a mean, low-down dog like you to get his hands on it." Grinning, the bounty hunter bent to pick up the weapon.

Harper began to mutter and moan. "Gold ... coffin full of gold ..."

"Eh? What's that you say?" The bounty hunter's curiosity was piqued, and he leaned closer. "What are you on about?"

"Buried gold ... I'll share it with you."

The bounty hunter holstered his pistol, grabbed Harper by his shirt, and yanked him up. "What gold?" He pressed the knife to Harper's throat.

"The gold in the grave."

"What grave?" The bounty hunter laughed. "You don't know which grave it's in, do you?"

"Sure I do." Harper pointed. "That one."

"Harper, you just made a very stupid mistake." The bounty hunter was unable to resist glancing in the direction Harper had indicated. It was all the opening Harper needed.

Whilst the bounty hunter's attention had been focused on the hand reaching for the bowie knife, Harper's other hand had grabbed Al Gibson's discarded skull. Now he took the opportunity to whack him with it.

The blow to the head caused the bounty hunter to sway, and his hold on Harper loosened. Harper got a cut to the throat, but it was not deep, and in his fury he did not even notice it. Another ferocious blow from the skull sent the bounty hunter sprawling. In an instant, Harper was on the dazed bounty hunter, pounding him with Gibson's skull.

When Gibson's skull finally broke, the red mist cleared from in front of Harper's eyes. The bounty hunter was out cold, his face a bloody pulp. "Told you, I wasn't gonna let you kill me, now, didn't I?"

Harper felt his throat. "You cut me, you bastard!" he declared, in some surprise. "Head hurts as well. Leastways, not as much as yours though, huh?" he said, fashioning bandages for his wounds from the bounty hunter's shirt.

"Now, what am I gonna do with you?" As he went through the bounty hunter's pockets, Harper pondered what to do with the insensible man. He found a cheroot. "Don't mind if I smoke, do you?"

Harper lit up, then rolled the unconscious bounty hunter into Gibson's grave.

As he filled in the grave, Harper considered his situation.

Franklin had cheated him, and now he would never know where the money was buried. Perhaps Franklin had even lied about it being buried in the cemetery. He wondered how long it would take to dig up every grave. "Too long," he said aloud, looking around him. "Lot of dead men."

His gaze alighted on the grave he had randomly pointed out to the bounty hunter. It looked no different to any of the others, apart from the name on the wooden cross.

Harper began to laugh wildly.

The name on this marker read: Cal Harper.

Was it possible?

"Only one way to find out." He gathered up his tools, and once again set to digging up a coffin.

Harper grunted in exertion, as he pulled on the rope that he'd fastened around the coffin. "Damn heavy." He almost laughed – heavy, that was a good sign.

Straining, he finally pulled the wooden box free of its burial pit.

Harper felt sure he had the right grave this time. "Thought you were being smart, hey, Franklin? Thought you could cheat me, huh?"

A sudden moaning disturbed Harper and he cast around looking for the source, his hand pulling his gun free. "Who's there?"

But there was no further sound, and he could see no one. Harper holstered his pistol, picked up the crowbar and returned his attention to the coffin.

"Oh, Jeezus!" Harper reeled back from the charnel stench that was released as he forced off the coffin lid.

Holding his nose against the smell, Harper stepped closer to the oblong box. He had not expected the coffin to be occupied by a body. Only the gold. The gold was there all right; still in the cloth bags it had been in when they had stolen it. The bags were packed tightly around a body.

Harper grunted. The corpse was naked and teeming with maggots. He felt sick but steeled himself for a closer look.

Despite the ruined and decayed flesh, the corpse was still recognisable. Harper staggered away and vomited. He had recognised the decomposing body of Brett Franklin.

Harper wiped his mouth on his sleeve. "How in the hell could that be possible?" He shook his head, bringing a burst of pain that made him wince. It couldn't be possible. It wasn't possible, he told himself.

Again, Harper heard that eerie moaning, and he span round, drawing his gun. No more bounty hunters were going to take him by surprise. But again there was no one there.

"All right." Harper took a step closer to the open coffin. Half expecting Brett Franklin to rise up, he kept his pistol aimed at the corpse.

But apart from the writhing of the maggots, there was no movement within the wooden box. He fired anyway, three bullets into the putrid remains of a man he had killed back in Youngerville.

"It ain't possible." Harper spat. "I don't know how you got here, Franklin, but one thing I do know is that you're dead." And just to make sure, he fired again, two more bullets into the corpse. "There, that should keep you resting in peace."

Hunkering down beside the coffin, Harper pulled out one of the cloth bags.

"Wouldn't surprise me, Franklin, if you tried to trick me and replace the gold with rocks." He hefted the bag in his hand, reassuringly it felt and weighed like gold coins. He shook it, and smiled, pleased by the sound of the coins jingling.

Harper opened the bag – it *was* full of gold coins. "Seems like I've done you an injustice, Franklin, old friend."

He retied the bag and began to remove the rest. "No use to a dead man, now, is it?"

With one bag remaining, a shadow fell across Harper, and he looked up. But once again there was no one to be seen. "Damn graveyard, getting' to me." Scanning the cemetery, he reached for the last bag, and felt a hand close on his wrist.

"What the ...?" Harper's face contorted in an expression of horror and disgust. The putrescent hand of the late Brett Franklin was gripping his wrist.

"Let go of me, dammit!" Harper tried to pull free, but the hold was firm. He tried to pry the corpse's fingers loose to no avail.

"How on earth?" On one of the fingers that grasped Harper's wrist was a gold ring – the ring that Franklin always wore. The ring that Harper had taken from Franklin's finger after he had killed him. Harper had not noticed it before, now he fumbled in his pockets with his free hand. And found that the ring had disappeared.

Harper drew his revolver, and aimed it at the corpse's head. "Damn you, Franklin, if you don't let go of me, I'll blast you to hell," Harper snarled.

The corpse remained impassive, and Harper began to laugh. "I already done that, ain't I?"

Suddenly Harper changed his hold on his gun, and furiously struck the cadaver's hand with the butt of the weapon. Again and again he rained blows upon it, and just as suddenly he stopped again. His wrist still imprisoned in the grasp of the corpse's hand.

"You think you've got me beat, don't you, you bastard?"

Looking around for some means of freeing himself, Harper spotted the shovel. He had cast it aside after uncovering the coffin. It was beyond the reach of his hand. So he lay flat on the ground and manoeuvred himself around trying to reach the tool by hooking it with his foot. Still it remained out of reach.

"The cemetery lies on the other side of that hill." Jeb Shelton pointed ahead.

"You think we'll—" The sound of a single shot interrupted Marshall Wes Procter's reply. "Come on," he yelled, spurring his horse forward.

"It's him all right." Procter confirmed.

The man in the grave still lived. But only just.

"Harper, can you hear me?" Procter leaned closer to the dying man.

Harper gasped for breath. "Franklin wouldn't let me go." Blood spluttered from his mouth. "Bastard had hold of me ... wouldn't let me go ... held my wrist tight ... couldn't break his hold." Harper's words were growing fainter now. "Bastard said he'd kill me ... couldn't escape ... but I cheated him of his vengeance ..." Procter thought Harper was trying to laugh. "Used a bullet on myself ..." With a bloody gurgle, Harper fell finally silent.

"What do you suppose happened, Marshall?" asked a puzzled Shelton.

Procter surveyed the scene. An open coffin with its dead occupant. Several bags of gold coins. A freshly dug grave, with a wooden marker that already bore the name of its *just-dead* occupant – Cal Harper.

"He said that Franklin had a hold of him, wouldn't let loose, and he couldn't break that hold." Procter shook his head.

"Hell!" Shelton looked in the coffin, and turned pale.

"Take a good look." Procter spat on the cemetery dirt. "That's the fate that awaits all of us."

Shelton had seen enough and stepped away. "But is that really Brett Franklin?"

The Marshall shrugged. "Hard to tell, body's too far gone to say for sure." Procter paused to light his pipe. "But hell," he continued, "I can't see how it can be. Brett Franklin's only been dead two weeks. Harper killed him in Youngerville, and he was buried there too."

Shelton frowned. "What I don't understand—"

Marshall Procter cut him off. "Best not to try. Reckon he was raving at the end there. And besides, they always called him Crazy Cal. I guess he really was."

TO SUMMON A FLESH-EATING DEMON

"*The Book of Setopholes*? Pah!" Professor Ernest Mellman snorted in derision. The archaeologist leaned back in his armchair. "Next you will be telling me, you believe in Lovecraft's *Necronomicon*!"

Professor Julius Greydin glared at his seated guest. "Don't be ridiculous, Mellman. Lovecraft's book is a mere fiction."

Mellman chuckled. "Oh, and *The Book of Setopholes* isn't?"

"Of course not," snapped Greydin.

Although the academics were aged similarly – in their fifties – they were quite different in appearance.

Professor Greydin stood by the fireplace smoking his pipe. He was a tall, slim, and rather handsome man, with sleek dark hair. His colleague was shorter and broader. He wore a large pair of glasses, and what little remained of his hair was white.

One other man was present – although he was many years their junior – one of their students named Tony Danziger. He was quietly examining some of the curious tribal masks that adorned one wall of Professor Greydin's study.

"Really, Julius, you know as well as I do that that book does not exist."

"That's where you're wrong, Mellman, *The Book of Setopholes* does exist," insisted Greydin.

Professor Mellman glanced at Tony Danziger, and winked. "Have you tried Arkham's Miskatonic University, Julius?"

Greydin did not bother to respond to his flippant comment.

"No, I'm sorry, Julius, but the only place it exists is in the minds of a few poor deluded souls." Professor Mellman chuckled again. "You're not one of those are you, Julius?"

"You'll eat those words before the week is out, Mellman."

"Well, I know I have a healthy appetite," Mellman slapped his ample belly, "and I'll try almost anything when it comes to food, but I doubt I'll find a few words very filling."

Greydin muttered, "Oh, you'll taste humble pie."

Tony Danziger – a fine example of youthful vitality – had been listening with interest. His curiosity in need of satisfying, and fearing that the professors would come to blows, the tall and broad-shouldered student decided that now was a good time to interrupt. He sat in one of the leather armchairs and asked, "Excuse my ignorance, but just what is this *Book of Setopholes*?"

Professor Mellman answered, "It's a fantasy. Haven't you been listening, Tony?"

"Pay no attention to him, Danziger. You are aware of course, that Plato tells us Solon learnt of Atlantis from an Egyptian priest." Greydin held up a decanter. "More brandy?"

"Of course." Mellman held out his glass.

Danziger nodded in response to both statement and question.

Greydin refilled their glasses, then began to pace the room. "*The Book of Setopholes* is a legendary book of knowledge written by an Egyptian priest. Among the wisdom it contains, is an account of Atlantis and its fate."

"You mean of its drowning?" Not surprisingly, the student was familiar with the story of the legendary island.

"Yes, but Setopholes tells us that the Atlanteans worshipped dark and evil gods, with unholy rites and human sacrifices. But then – for some unknown reason – they gave up their bloody worship of these foul beings. It was then that Atlantis was drowned by the waves of the sea, as a punishment for turning away from their evil gods," explained Professor Greydin.

"Hmm," Danziger considered this. "A slight difference from Plato's account then."

Professor Mellman poured himself another glass of brandy, and said, "Ah, but that's not all is it, Julius?"

"You've probably assumed that Setopholes was the name of the Egyptian priest, but you would be wrong. His name is lost to us," continued the anthropology professor.

The student asked, "Then who, or what, was Setopholes?"

Professor Greydin went on, "He was the man who told the nameless priest all of the arcane knowledge contained in the book."

"Come on man; get to the best bit," Mellman urged.

"All right, all right, Mellman, I'm coming to it." Greydin glared at his colleague.

"Setopholes was a wizard who passed on his wisdom to the priest, by the use of a spell, and the knowledge was revealed to the priest in his dreams."

Unable to restrain himself, Mellman interrupted, "But the best part of this fantastic tale is that the things the priest learnt from these spell-sent dreams happened on another world."

Greydin again glared at the archaeologist.

"Isn't that the most outrageous thing you've ever heard, Tony?" Mellman laughed. "No, wait a minute, what's more outrageous is that anyone would believe such a thing could possibly be true."

Unwilling to offend either professor, the student remained quiet.

As did a scowling Greydin.

"But of course it's all a hoax," said Mellman.

"So, just what is the origin of this book, then?"

"There are references to it in a Victorian book called *Mysteries of Dark Wisdom*; you have a copy haven't you, Julius?"

"Of course I have," Greydin replied. "Would you like to see it?" he asked Danziger.

"Yes, Professor, I would."

As Professor Greydin went to retrieve it from one of the many bookcases contained in the room, Mellman went on, "It claims that there were translations and copies of *The Book of Setopholes* made through the ages, among them Greek and Latin, and even some medieval copies. Unfortunately for Julius, this Victorian book is universally considered – not to put too fine a point on it

129

– a load of old tosh." Mellman laughed again.

Greydin grunted. "Huh! That's what you think." The anthropologist had taken the book to his desk.

"Not just me, old boy." Mellman remained where he sat, but Danziger went to take a look.

"This is Charles Roland's, *Mysteries of Dark Wisdom*, published in eighteen ninety," Greydin said, pride evident in his voice. "Not many copies survive."

"Charles Roland? I've never heard of him," admitted Danziger.

"Few have," Greydin conceded. "And to be honest, little is known about the man himself. He was born in eighteen forty-three and died, or at least, was last seen in nineteen o seven. But what is certain, is that he was an expert on the occult."

Professor Mellman snorted again. "Hah! He was a charlatan and a crank."

"Few men have dared delve as deeply into such matters as Roland," contended Professor Greydin.

"This book is a compendium of sorcery and the occult, but its primary interest is the information it provides upon *The Book of Setopholes*," Greydin explained.

"So, apart from Atlantis being on another world, what else is in *The Book of Setopholes*?" Danziger turned the pages of the Victorian book carefully.

"It's a collection of magical spells and rituals, information on gods and demons, and records of the history and events of Setopholes's world."

Professor Greydin ignored Mellman's snort. "Roland intended to publish a translation of *The Book of Setopholes*, and a more detailed book about it and its contents. Alas neither was to appear."

"Bloody good job if you ask me." Professor Mellman's opinion was scathing, "Roland was no more than a mere writer of fiction, and not very good fiction at that."

"Well, I for one would like to read it," said Danziger. "May I borrow this please, Professor?"

Greydin was pleased that the student was showing such an interest. "Yes, but please be careful with it."

"I will; don't worry."

Mellman groaned, "Oh, for goodness sake, Tony, you don't want to be wasting your time reading that."

The clock struck the hour – ten o'clock.

The student smiled. "Speaking of time, it's time I was off."

"Yes, me too, Julius. Thanks for the brandy, excellent as always. I will see you tomorrow."

"It's been an interesting evening, Professor Greydin. Thank you. And don't worry about your book, I'll return it in a couple of days, if that's okay?"

"Yes, that's fine. And I may have something very important to tell you then."

"Oh?" Mellman's curiosity was aroused. "And what might that be?"

But despite Mellman's enquiry, Greydin would say no more on the matter and wished his guests goodnight.

Student and professor shared the same route for part of their journey to their respective homes.

"Well, what do you suppose that was all about, Professor?"

Professor Mellman smiled. "Can't you guess?"

"I've really no idea."

"You know; Julius has never been married?"

"No, I didn't know that," admitted Danziger. "Do you mean he intends to announce his engagement?"

Mellman shook his head. "It's rare for Julius to let someone borrow one of his precious books."

Professor Mellman's apparent change of subject had Danziger puzzled.

"He likes you, young Tony."

"You mean ...?" Danziger was dumfounded, momentarily lost for words. "Just what are you suggesting, Professor?"

"Suggesting? Was I suggesting something? Ah, I have to go this way now, and much as I'd like to continue our conversation, it's much too chilly for me to hang around here. I'm off home, young Tony. No, I'm none the wiser than you. We'll just have to wait and see what revelation Julius has to make."

A couple of days later an uncomfortable Tony Danziger was back in Julius Greydin's study. He had only intended returning the professor's book, but Greydin had insisted he come in. Professor Mellman was again sitting by the fire.

"Well, Julius what's this all about?" Mellman asked, once Danziger had joined them.

"I told you last time you were here, that I might have an important announcement to make."

Danziger looked worried. He had assumed that with Professor Mellman present there would be no embarrassing declaration by Professor Greydin. Surely, the professor was not going to reveal that he was in love with him in front of his colleague.

Greydin spoke, "As Mellman knows, I have been searching for many years, for what I suppose you could call my heart's desire. It has proved to be a most elusive search; one that I feared would never find fulfilment. But now, and I can scarcely believe it, my quest has come to an end."

Danziger glanced at Professor Mellman. Mellman smiled back.

"After all this time I have finally found it." Professor Greydin paused dramatically, before announcing, "Gentlemen, I have *The Book of Setopholes*."

The student breathed a sigh of relief; he thought he saw

Mellman wink at him. The old devil had been kidding him all along!

Mellman was saying, "Really, Julius, you don't expect us to believe you've managed to locate a copy of that damned book, do you?"

"Not just found, Mellman. I have it. Well, don't just sit there come and see; you too, Danziger," urged Greydin, unlocking one of his desk's drawers.

From the drawer he carefully removed a large book, and gently laid it upon the desk. The other men gathered round. The ironbound book was easily identifiable of being of great antiquity.

"My God!" Mellman gasped.

Greydin opened the book turning to the title page. "This is what you have refused to believe in for more years than I care to remember, Mellman. This is probably the only surviving copy of the only printed edition of the legendary *Book of Setopholes*," he announced, his tone reverential.

For once Mellman was speechless. It was left to Danziger to ask, "Where on earth did you get it, Professor?"

Greydin was reluctant to reveal how he had come by the book, "A dealer in antiquities and antiquarian books that I know located it for me. But that's not important, what is important is that the book exists," was all he would say.

Danziger had read all about the different editions of *The Book of Setopholes*, but he had never expected to see one. Especially not the printed version of 1510.

The book was nearly five hundred years old, and had been included on the Index of Forbidden Books by Pope Paul IV in 1559. Quite naturally, it was not in good condition, but it was a miracle it had survived at all.

Neither Mellman nor Danziger pressed Greydin for further information on his acquisition of the book; they were too eager to see what was printed on its fabled pages.

At first, Mellman was convinced the book was a fake, but reluctantly he had to admit, "Well, Julius it appears to be genuine. Though of course it will have to be analysed to prove whether it is or not."

Although Danziger did not know much Latin, especially that of Renaissance Italy, the three men studied the ancient tome late into the night. The student having to content himself with the translations made by the other men, and the grotesque woodcuts that illustrated the book.

"The book may date to the sixteenth century, but that doesn't mean that there's any truth to what's written in it," Mellman pointed out.

"Ever the sceptic, Mellman."

"Of course, my dear fellow. But just because the book exists, it doesn't mean that this story of Atlantis being on another world has any validity."

Mellman paused a moment in thought, and his grin grew broader. "What if we were to put some of this arcane knowledge to the test?"

"What do you mean?" Greydin asked.

"Why, a spell of course, Julius. It won't prove anything about Atlantis ever having existed on another planet, but there's no reason why we couldn't attempt one of these so-called magical rituals from this book of yours."

"Well, I'm not sure we should—" Professor Greydin began.

Mellman interrupted, "Come now, Julius, think of it as an experiment."

"But these things should not just be gone into lightly," protested Greydin.

"Quit stalling, Julius. Anyone would think you were afraid your book is about to be exposed as the usual hotchpotch of unworkable nonsense that all these grimoires invariably are. What say you, Tony?"

"Well ..."

Not giving the student time to finish speaking, Professor Mellman continued, "Have you so little faith after all in your book of marvellous magics, Julius?"

"I really don't think—"

Mellman interrupted again, "Yes, you're right, of course, we'd only be wasting our time."

Greydin sighed. "Very well," he reluctantly agreed.

"Splendid! Then if we reconvene here tomorrow evening about nine? That will give you plenty of time to select one of the rituals, and make whatever preparations are necessary."

"Very well, that suits me."

Mellman looked at the student. "Well, how about you, Tony?"

"Me?" Danziger had not expected to be included.

"Yes, of course you'll join us," Professor Greydin insisted.

"Then in that case, yes, I'll be here."

It was approaching nine o'clock when Tony Danziger arrived at Professor Greydin's house. He had thought about backing out and instead asking Michelle Chalmers – one of his fellow students – out on a date. But he was hoping to go on one of Professor Mellman's archaeological expeditions, and so he thought he had better appear keen – even though Mellman was not Danziger's favourite person right now.

He had to admit that he was curious about what would happen when they tried one of the so-called spells from that mouldy old book – probably nothing, but wouldn't it be something if it did.

The student smiled – perhaps there would be a spell he could cast on Professor Mellman – a day or two as a frog might do the professor some good.

Just as Danziger reached the top of the steps to Greydin's front door, it started to rain. Danziger reached out and rapped on the door with the gargoyle-shaped knocker. He did not have to wait long for the door to open.

As usual, Professor Mellman had arrived first. "Tony, at last! What kept you? I was beginning to think you had changed your mind about joining us." He handed the student a glass of brandy. "Julius refused to reveal what tonight's act of necromancy is, until you arrived."

"I'm sorry I kept you waiting," the student apologised, although he was not late, and he felt that if anyone should be offering apologies it was Professor Mellman.

However, Mellman was oblivious of the student's mood.

"Really, Mellman, I have no intention of indulging in necromancy." Greydin paused dramatically, then said, "At least not yet."

Mellman was taken aback. "You're not serious?"

Professor Greydin smiled.

Danziger laughed. "You should have seen your face, Professor."

"Well, yes, I knew you were joking really," the archaeologist blustered.

Greydin's smile had quickly vanished. "Enough levity. We must be about our business."

"And just what is our business, Julius? What dark rite have you in mind to perform tonight?" enquired Professor Mellman.

"A summoning," was the reply.

"A summoning? Are you sure?"

"Of course I'm sure."

"That's only about one step removed from necromancy, isn't it?"

"Demonology, my dear Mellman."

"Well, I'm surprised you've chosen such an ambitious venture, old man. I would have thought you would have chosen something a bit simpler. Something like a love spell for instance. What do you think, Tony?"

Danziger frowned, "I'm sure Professor Greydin knows what he's doing."

"Will you stop prattling, Mellman?"

"Prattle? Do I prattle?"

"Mellman!"

"Oh, very well, old boy. Let's get on with it then, shall we?"

Mellman and Danziger finished their drinks and followed Greydin out of the room. He led them along the oak-panelled hallway towards the rear of the house. "I thought we would make use of the basement," Greydin explained as he opened a door. "More room, and it seemed more appropriate."

The three men descended into a large cellar.

The centre of the room had been cleared, boxes and crates lined the walls; another door led out of the room.

"Behold the lair of the sorcerer," Mellman declared in a stentorian voice.

On the floor a pentagram had been drawn in red and purple chalk, a lectern stood outside the pentagram between two points of the star.

"Is that where you keep your wine?" Mellman pointed at the other door.

"Never mind that, Mellman, you've had enough to drink already," Greydin snapped.

Outside thunder rumbled ominously. "Ho, a portentous omen." Mellman laughed.

Danziger asked, "What exactly are you planning to do in this experiment, Professor Greydin?"

"Apart from make a fool of yourself," Mellman whispered to Danziger.

The student could not help smiling at Mellman's comment.

"I have chosen a ritual that will prove *The Book of Selopholes* is a genuine work of magical knowledge."

"And what ritual is that?"

"Really, Tony, I sometimes think you go around with cotton wool stuffed in your ears. Julius already told us he plans to summon a demon, no less."

"It's entitled 'How to Summon a Flesh-Eating Demon'," Professor Greydin announced, opening the book that lay upon the lectern.

"Is there any other kind, old man? Have you ever heard of a vegetarian-demon, Tony?"

"Er, no." Danziger was beginning to feel foolish.

"If we do summon anything, I insist on checking it out to make sure you haven't got one of your students to dress up to play the part. I'm sure you could get that fool Brown to do that."

Danziger felt that, of the two professors, only Mellman would resort to such an act.

Professor Greydin was becoming irritated by his colleague's comments, "Will you take this seriously, Mellman?"

Danziger did not know why the two men spent so much of their time together, Mellman was continually trying to provoke Professor Greydin, and he usually succeeded.

"Right you are. Well then, Aleister Crowley, let's get on with it," urged Mellman, eager to complete the ritual and thus have Greydin fail.

"What do we have to do, Professor?" Danziger was also eager to get things over with.

"Stand at the points of the star." Professor Greydin pointed in turn to the points to the left and right of him, "Stay outside the pentagram, don't walk through it," he commanded.

From the lectern, Greydin took two pieces of paper and handed one to each of the men.

The student puzzled over what was written on the paper. "What's this, Professor?"

"It's your part in the ceremony. When I give the signal the pair of you chant the incantation written there."

"Chant it?" Mellman looked doubtful. "I can't even understand it. It's just gibberish."

"Probably the Atlantean equivalent of abracadabra." Danziger grinned.

"Hocus-pocus," muttered Mellman. "What's the betting Julius fails to even conjure up a white rabbit?"

Ignoring Mellman, Greydin turned to the other door, opened it and went through.

"Where are you going now?" Mellman wanted to know.

Greydin did not answer.

"Of course, the wine cellar! A bottle of your finest vintage, Julius."

Greydin returned, carrying a small crate. He opened it, and pulled out a black chicken.

Mellman asked, "What on earth are you doing with that thing?"

"It's the sacrifice of course," answered Greydin.

"You're not serious, are you, Professor?" Danziger was shocked.

"Of course I am. Now let's begin shall we?"

"Yes," Mellman concurred. "Let the ceremony begin."

Professor Greydin picked up a knife that lay beside the book. He held the struggling chicken above the centre of the pentagram.

"My God, man!" Mellman cried, as Greydin deftly wielded the knife, and allowed the chicken's blood to spill onto the floor. Mellman and Danziger watched in distaste.

"There we are. Simple," Greydin left the chicken lying in the widening pool of its blood. "That should do it."

Danziger asked, "What now?"

"Quiet, both of you," Greydin ordered.

Professor Greydin began to read aloud an incantation he had translated from *The Book of Setopholes*. He spoke in a commanding voice, "Oh, hear me, creature of the pit. I, your master, Julius Greydin speak. Accept the Red Offering. I summon. You must obey. Come to me. Obey my command!" Greydin continued speaking, chanting strange words that neither Mellman nor Danziger recognised.

Greydin pointed the bloody knife at his acolytes, his signal for them to join in.

Mellman and Danziger looked at each other, and then feeling somewhat foolish took up their part in the incantation – chanting more of the strange words.

Greydin continued to speak for about five minutes repeating the incantation.

Mellman had had enough. "Well, Julius, you've tried your best, but you've got to admit ..."

An incredibly loud boom of thunder drowned out his words, the house shook as if it had been struck and the light went out.

"Jesus!" Danziger swore.

"Good grief!" Mellman cried. "That must have been close."

Greydin was performing the incantation again, but shouting the words now. The light flickered back into life, but the pentagram remained empty.

Professor Greydin fell silent.

"Look upon it as a valuable experiment. You've conclusively proved that magic does not work. You tried your best, but it was never going to succeed," said Mellman, trying to console his colleague.

The three men were back in the study. Greydin was slumped in his chair; head held in his hands. Danziger refilling their glasses.

Mellman added some coal to the fire. "Although I'll admit for a moment, even I thought it was going to work."

"No, Mellman, it was my fault the ritual failed. I allowed myself to be pressured by you. I should have been more patient: these things work better at their appointed times. In my eagerness to prove you wrong I adapted the ritual as I thought fit. Next time I will perform it correctly."

"Next time?" Mellman questioned. "You're not serious, are you, Julius?"

"But of course. I intend to try again."

"Julius, you proved that sorcery does not work, that demons do not exist."

"My first attempt was flawed; it cannot be considered a legitimate attempt. I must try again."

"Julius, give it up," Mellman urged.

"I must make one more attempt. I have to perform the ritual again, but next time I must do it precisely as it is written in *The Book of Setopholes*. Though I do not expect either of you to attend."

Tony Danziger had had no intention of attending Professor Greydin's next attempt at demonology. Instead, he asked Michelle Chalmers for that date, and she had accepted his invitation to go to the cinema. But when the night in question arrived, she never showed up. After waiting for her for an hour, Danziger finally had to admit he had been stood up.

At a loose end, the student found himself, somewhat reluctantly, at Professor Greydin's house again.

For a change, he had arrived before Professor Mellman.

"Can you follow this, Danziger?" Professor Greydin handed the student a piece of paper.

The student examined what was written on the paper.

"No! Don't even mouth the words," Greydin warned. "You understand it?"

"Yes, I think so." Not that he understood the meaning of the words.

"Good. Would you care for a drink?"

"Please."

"This spell certainly seems to me to be medieval in origin. So tonight we perform the ceremony in the original Latin."

Professor Greydin poured Danziger a drink.

"Learn the incantation, but remember do not utter it until I say so. Now, if you will excuse me, I have some things to prepare."

When Professor Greydin returned, he made an unexpected demand that shocked the student. "Get undressed, there's a good fellow."

"What?" Danziger spluttered.

"Put this on." Greydin threw him a long, red, hooded robe. "We're doing this rite right this time." The professor smiled briefly. "Don't worry we'll all be wearing them. I'm going upstairs to change into mine now."

Both men had changed into their scarlet cowls when Professor Mellman arrived.

"Hello? What's this?" Mellman grinned. "'The Masque of the Red Death'?"

"Here you are, Mellman." Greydin handed him one of the garments. "I want you to wear this."

"What's all this nonsense then?"

"As I said, this time we do the ritual exactly as it says in the book."

"Have you got a bushy white beard for me then?"

Greydin sighed. "What are you on about now?"

"So I can be Father Christmas, of course."

"Have you been drinking?"

"Just a tipple, old boy. Why? Are you offering?"

"Just get changed."

"Oh, very well. If you insist."

"I do."

Mellman went upstairs to change. And Danziger wondered, somewhat concerned, how Professor Greydin would react, when the ritual failed again.

Mellman joined them again in the study. "Well, how do I look?"

"Good. I was worried it wouldn't fit." Greydin glanced at the clock. "It'll soon be midnight, high time we got on with things."

Mellman eyed the drinks cabinet. "Isn't there time for a drink?"

"No. I have calculated that midnight is the optimum time to attempt this ceremony." Greydin opened the door to the cellar.

"Now, down to the basement, both of you. And put up your hoods."

Mellman led the way, Danziger went next, Professor Greydin followed, locking the cellar door before going down the staircase.

"So, what else are we doing differently this time, Julius?" Mellman asked as they descended. "Oh! I see." He had reached the bottom of the stairs.

Danziger expressed his surprise more forcefully, "Bloody hell!"

Instead of the electric light this time the cellar was lit by smoky candles that stood on skulls – most were animal, but some looked decidedly human. Black drapes covered the walls, hiding the assorted clutter that was stored in the cellar.

Mellman gestured at the skulls. "Where on earth did you get those, Julius?"

"For heaven's sake, from the biology department of course. You don't think I've been grave robbing, do you?"

"Isn't this all a bit *Hammer House of Horror*, Professor?" asked Danziger.

"I'm following the instructions to the letter this time. Even if it means using all this paraphernalia."

"Well, I must say it's very atmospheric." Mellman was scrutinising a skull. "Monkey?" he queried.

Greydin nodded. "The others are, cat, dog, sheep, goat, horse, and bull, and those three are, of course, human: male, female, and child," he indicated each in turn.

"Take up your positions as before." Greydin instructed, crossing the room, pulling back a drape to reveal the cellar's other door.

Mellman groaned. "Not another unfortunate chicken."

Danziger whispered to Mellman, "Judging by the lengths Professor Greydin is going to, I expect he's got the other ten members of his coven waiting in there."

"You may be right, Tony." Mellman replied, as Greydin returned accompanied by another red-robed acolyte. Face hidden by the hood of their robe, this fourth person moved slowly and unsteadily. As Mellman had predicted Professor Greydin was again carrying the small crate containing a chicken.

"Aren't you going to introduce us, Julius?"

Danziger was concerned about the new participant. "Is he all right?"

"Has he been partaking of your wine cellar?"

Greydin put the crate down, then leaned close to his companion, and whispered instructions.

Obeying, the newcomer moved to the middle of the pentagram, and allowed their red robe to fall to the ground – to reveal their identity, and their nakedness.

"My God!" exclaimed Mellman, averting his eyes.

Danziger gasped, amazed, "Michelle! What are you doing here?"

Michelle did not reply, just smiled vaguely.

Mellman pulled Greydin to one side. "Julius, what is the meaning of this?"

Greydin shrugged. "She is a vital component of tonight's ceremony."

"She's been drugged!" Danziger had picked up Michelle's

robe, and was trying to get her to put it back on.

"So, she's not doing this willingly?" Mellman accused.

"Hardly. I couldn't very well advertise for a young virgin to take part in a black magic ritual, could I?"

"But that's monstrous!" Mellman was appalled. "Now look here, Julius, I cannot allow this to proceed."

"Why ever not?" Greydin was surprised by his friend's attitude.

"You don't seriously expect us to allow you to sacrifice this girl do you?"

"Sacrifice? Really, Mellman, don't be so absurd. Do you really think I'm going to plunge my knife into this young girl's heaving bosom?" Greydin snorted. "Now who's being all *Hammer House of Horror*?"

Mellman asked, "Then just what is Miss Chalmers role in all of this?"

"Yeah, just what are you intending, Professor?" Danziger snarled.

"Calm down, both of you. She is part of the lure to bring the demon into our dimension. The scent of the chicken's blood and virgin flesh, don't you see?"

Danziger was angry. "And what's to stop the demon from devouring her when it obeys the summons?"

"The creature will be disorientated on appearing, I have only to speak the word of power, and the creature will be utterly under my command." Greydin smiled. "She will come to no harm, and will remember nothing."

Mellman shook his head. "Have you taken leave of your senses?"

"I won't allow it. It's too risky."

"I don't need your permission, Danziger."

Danziger's hands were clenched fists. "What about Michelle's permission? You haven't got that either. You could be charged with kidnapping."

Mellman pulled the student away. "Calm down, Tony. It's all right. No harm will come to Miss Chalmers. After all it's not as if the incantation is going to work now, is it?" He smiled reassuringly. "She'll be perfectly safe."

"God! How stupid of me. You're right, of course. All of this black magic paraphernalia had me thinking it might actually work. Talk about getting carried away, it's just that I really like Michelle, the thought of anything happening to her ..." The student shrugged, embarrassed.

"I understand, but she'll be fine."

"Nevertheless, he shouldn't be doing this without Michelle's say so."

"Please, Tony; I think it will be better if we let Julius carry on. No harm can come to Michelle; I assure you. As for Julius, he is obviously unwell; I'm worried what he will do if we try to prevent this going ahead."

The student considered, and decided that Mellman was right. There was no real danger to Michelle if they carried on with what he now realised was a madman's farce, but there was no knowing how Greydin would react if they attempted to prevent him enacting this ritual. "Okay then, Professor, but he's crazy, and you better make sure he sees a shrink."

"Don't worry; I'll make sure he gets the help he needs."

"Well? Are you two taking part?" demanded Greydin, impatient to begin.

Mellman looked at Danziger. "Tony?"

The student nodded in response.

"Very well, Julius."

"Good," said Greydin. "Then let us proceed."

Naked, Michelle lay in the pentagram, head and limbs corresponding with the five points of the star. Mellman and Danziger each stood by her hands, whilst Greydin stood at her

146

head.

As before Greydin sacrificed the chicken, allowing the blood to flow freely onto Michelle's body and splashing himself in the process.

Michelle writhed and groaned softly.

Tony realised how aroused he was, and hoped neither of the other men would notice. He was thankful that candles rather than the more powerful electric light lit the room at that moment.

But in the light of the candles, the blood-splattered Julius Greydin looked decidedly sinister. The student had doubts about the man's sanity, and had second thoughts about allowing him to continue. Would it be worse to try to stop this now or let it proceed, only for Greydin to fail in his sorcery?

Professor Greydin began to read the incantation, speaking first the words in Latin, and then the strange words of an unknown language.

Mellman started chanting at Greydin's signal, but Danziger missed it, joining in slightly after the professor. The student was unable to keep his gaze from the beautiful Michelle's bloodstained body.

Mellman realised he was sweating. It seemed unnaturally hot, and there was an unpleasant smell coming from somewhere. Yes, the air smelt decidedly sulphurous.

Suddenly darkness descended as the candles went out, inexplicably extinguished. Professor Greydin stopped speaking in mid-sentence.

Something growled.

"Julius? What was —?" Mellman's sudden scream was shrill.

Danziger shouted, "What the hell?" as something wet splashed him. "The lights, Professor. Where's the light switch?" He started to move towards the foot of the stairs; taking a chance on a light switch being there. He collided with someone. "Professor Greydin is that you?" Or something!

Danziger staggered away from whatever he had bumped into. Groping in front of him, he found the wall, running his hands over its surface he found the light switch. He flicked it on, and turned around.

Professor Greydin was crouched over the fallen Mellman; there was more blood on the floor than just the chicken's. There was no sign of a demon.

"What the hell happened, Professor?"

Professor Greydin turned and looked up. He was drenched in blood, his mouth smeared crimson. Greydin stared at the student, chewing on something as he did so, drool dribbling from between his lips.

"Jesus!" Danziger caught a glimpse of Mellman; blood spilled freely from the gaping wound in the archaeologist's neck. "Oh my God!" he gasped.

In horror, Danziger began to back up the stairs; Greydin had been so obsessed with summoning a demon that he had finally flipped. Then he remembered Michelle – he could not leave her at the mercy of a madman.

Greydin ripped Mellman's robe open, stroking a hand over the archaeologist's plump belly, watching the student as he did so.

Danziger slowly came back down the stairs. Michelle lay oblivious. Greydin swallowed, then bent his head and began lapping at Mellman's blood.

Danziger edged his way around Greydin. "It's okay, Professor; me and Michelle are leaving now."

The student crouched down next to Michelle, warily watching the professor, afraid that at any moment the lunatic would leap at him.

Michelle opened her eyes, "Oh, hi Tony," she said, slurring her words. "Where am I?" she mumbled, a confused expression on her face.

Danziger smiled at her, "It's all right, Michelle. I'll soon have you out of here."

Michelle's eyes closed again.

Greydin raised Mellman's limp arm, and sank his teeth into the flesh, chomping noisily.

Danziger lifted Michelle, and began to rise. Greydin snarled. The student paused a moment, then continued to stand up. Greydin snarled again, releasing Mellman's arm.

Danziger crouched back down, lowering Michelle gently to the floor. The student considered the situation. Obviously, Greydin was not about to let him take Michelle. Would the professor let him go alone? Could he risk it? Would Michelle be safe? There was plenty more meat left on Professor Mellman, enough for the maniac to dine on, surely he would not need to start on Michelle. There had to be enough time to get help. He had to try. Then he saw Greydin's knife. It lay discarded on the floor. Of course, he could always overpower the professor. Greydin was in shape for an old guy, but he would be no match for the student. But just in case, he began to reach for the sacrificial weapon.

Greydin watched him, smiling again, and still gobbling human flesh – pieces of Professor Ernest Mellman.

"You crazy bastard," Danziger muttered. The student felt sick.

The knife was almost in his grasp when Greydin leapt at him. Danziger was fit and healthy, and physically Greydin's superior, or at least he should have been. He struggled against the elder man who was possessed a strength far greater than a man his age should have.

Danziger was grappled to the ground. There was no trace of the professor in the man who lowered his face towards him. Madness shone in his eyes; the mouth came closer to Danziger's throat. His teeth were fangs, and he could smell the foulness of the possessed man's breath.

The student screamed as he felt searing pain in his body –

nails grown sharp and long, ripping and tearing through his bloody red robe and lacerating his chest.

Danziger locked a hand in a stranglehold around Greydin's throat, and squeezed. And squeezed. His other hand scrabbled for the knife.

And then it was in his hand, and again and again he stabbed, plunging the blade into the professor's back.

The professor howled, and the student managed to throw his tutor off. Greydin landed with a crash in a pile of splintering crates.

Gasping for breath, Danziger realised that incredibly Greydin was rising. The student got to his feet, and ran up the stairs. He told himself he was not running away but luring Greydin away from Michelle.

Behind him he could hear the professor in pursuit, could almost feel the maniac's breath on the back of his neck. He reached the top of the steps and the door, he turned the handle, but the door was stuck and refused to open.

He clawed frantically at the door, then remembered Professor Greydin had locked it. The student threw himself at the door in a desperate attempt to force it open. Then Greydin was upon him; the professor had launched himself up the last few steps.

For a brief moment, the two men struggled at the top of the flight, then they fell, hurtling down the staircase.

Falling together, Danziger screamed in agony, as five sharp points tore through his robe and skin, piercing and ripping the flesh of his stomach. He hit the stone floor first; Greydin fell atop him and was cushioned from the impact.

The possessed man reared above the stunned student. For the first time since performing the spell, Professor Greydin spoke, or rather growled, "Not Greydin. Not professor. Am Karkasoz." And then he made a sound that might have been laughter. "Am hungry!"

Groggily, Danziger tried to evade the next attack. He was

unsuccessful, shrieking in agony as Greydin lashed at his face, sharp claws tearing at his eyes.

Yelling, Danziger flailed blindly with the dagger, stabbing frenziedly.

It was the screaming that made him stop. Danziger realised that there was someone else screaming. Someone other than himself – Michelle.

He pushed Greydin's unmoving body off and slowly rose.

"Michelle? It's all right. It's all over."

"Keep away." He was unaware that Michelle cowered on the floor, trembling, frightened. She did not know where she was, or what had happened to her. "Just stay away from me."

Guided by the sound of her voice, Danziger staggered blindly towards her.

His robe so tattered he was virtually naked, bloodstained and bruised, face ruined, flaps of skin hanging loose, Danziger was a hideous and terrifying apparition.

Michelle was backing away from him. "You're insane; keep away from me." She was sobbing. "You've killed Professor Mellman and Professor Greydin. And God only knows what you've done to me."

"No, that was Greydin. I saved you."

"You're a liar and a murderer!" she shouted. "I saw you kill Greydin."

"The ritual worked," Danziger tried to explain to an uncomprehending Michelle. "Greydin wasn't mad. He summoned the demon; only it possessed him. He must have meant it to possess you, but it didn't, it took his body instead. I wonder why."

He had a sudden realisation, remembered something Professor Greydin had said about why Michelle was a vital requirement for the ritual. Danziger laughed wildly – Michelle was not a virgin. But apparently, Professor Greydin had been.

THE STROMBOLLI COLLECTION

"Bastard!" Celine Dupont slapped George Petit's cheek, spun on her heel and with head held high she walked from the room.

Petit stood, naked, red-faced and fuming, watching her depart.

From where she lay – also nude – upon Petit's four-poster bed, Anne Evard had observed Celine's arrival, shocked outrage at the other woman's presence, and her angry departure, with mounting amusement. As the door slammed closed behind the girl, Anne was unable to hold back her laughter any longer. Much to Petit's annoyance.

"Shut up!" Petit snapped, without turning to look at her. "Bitch!" he added, although it was unclear to which woman he referred. Perhaps it was both.

Celine was furious. She had received a note inviting her to a romantic assignation at Petit's house. She had not anticipated finding Petit sharing his bed with that brazen whore, nor that she was expected to join them. Her fury was at Petit; the older, more-experienced woman, and at her own self. 'Foolish girl', Petit had called her. Anne Evard had described her as an 'Unsophisticated child'. Celine knew Petit's reputation as a womanizer. Yet she had been so flattered by his interest. How could she have been so stupid? She should never have accepted the invitation.

And now here she was, walking home, all alone. Celine shivered, pulled her shawl tighter and hurried on. Although the night was chill, it was more than the weather that caused her to shudder.

A lunatic was terrorising Paris, attacking young women. Pretty young women like Celine Dupont.

There were footsteps behind her, Celine paused, looked

around. She could see no one on the street.

"Who's there?" Celine called. "George, is it you?" she said, hoping Petit had followed. Had come to beg her forgiveness.

There was no response to her query.

"Stupid!" She berated herself for thinking like a romantic, lovesick girl again.

Celine turned back at another noise from somewhere further along the road. She peered into the shadows. Was there someone lurking? She gave a cry as a large rat emerged from a pile of garbage and scurried across the street into another.

Again she heard the footsteps coming from behind. They were definitely getting closer.

She heard a voice call out. "Where are you?" It was male, but harsh, not the cultured tone she would recognise as being George's. Spotting Celine, the man hailed her. "Mademoiselle, wait!"

Celine turned to see a man approaching. Poorly dressed, he was clearly searching for someone or something, looking from side to side; every now and then he would stoop and stare intently into the gloom.

"Have you seen him?"

Celine shook her head. "I have seen no one."

"My rat. I must find him."

"Oh. I see." Celine was on the brink of giggling, but his next comment killed her sudden amusement.

"My family will starve if I do not."

"Black, was he?" She held her hands slightly apart. "About so big?"

The man nodded.

"He went that way." She pointed to where the rat had run.

Without a word of thanks the man hurried to where she had indicated, went to his knees and started tossing aside bits of trash, desperately searching for the rodent.

Celine shuddered and started walking again. Perhaps there

was someone who wanted to buy the rat – though she could not think why – and the man intended to buy food for his family with the money he would get for the creature. The alternative was too horrible to think of. She considered herself fortunate that it had not occurred to the man to rob her.

She walked even quicker now, frequently glancing over her shoulder, in case the rat-catcher gave up on his search and came after easier pickings. Increasing her pace, Celine almost ran into the man who stepped from out of the dark into her path. Judging by the fine clothes that he wore the fellow was evidently a gentleman of some means.

"Oh, monsieur, you startled me."

Anton Jacques smiled. "Well, now. What have we here?"

From his tone, and the predatory look in his eye, Celine knew she should run, but the man's reactions were quicker, and he grabbed her before she could do so.

"Get off me!" The girl struggled, tried to scratch at his face.

"A pretty thing." He thrust her roughly up against a wall.

Celine groaned.

"I like pretty things." He punched her in the stomach, and she bent double in pain. "Like to hurt them." Jacques pulled her up straight again by her blonde hair. "Like to fuck 'em too!" He pressed himself against the terrified girl, a hand finding its way inside her dress and squeezing a breast; his mouth planting a slobbering kiss upon her unwilling lips.

"Get off her!" Much to his consternation, Jacques found himself pulled from the girl.

"How dare you?" he snarled angrily at the newcomer who had dared to intervene. "She's mine!"

His tone cooled as he got a better look at the man who had come to Celine's rescue. He did not seem concerned by Jacques's aggressive manner. This was a man who had clearly lived a hard life and was no stranger to violence. A wiry individual that could have been handsome once, but now his features were ugly and menacing. His nose had obviously been broken at some time in the past and his mouth was missing several teeth. Like his face, his clothes had seen better days. His body odour was unpleasant and his breath smelt strongly of alcohol.

Jacques already found himself stepping away from the man. It was the smell, he told himself.

"Leave her alone." It was said calmly.

"Piss off, you filthy tramp!" Jacques weighed up his chances. He was younger, healthier, than the girl's rescuer, but ultimately he was a bully who targeted women and weaklings. The man who advanced towards him threateningly was clearly a different matter altogether.

Besides, the man had allowed Jacques a glimpse of the knife he had concealed under his jacket.

Jacques kept backing away. He glanced to his left; there was an alley there that ultimately would take him to an inn he sometimes frequented. A drink was what he needed. "Keep her!" Jacques snapped, as he stepped into the alleyway. Calling out, "A dirty whore for a filthy tramp!" as he dashed away.

The man returned to where Celine Dupont remained cowering against the wall.

"He is gone." He held out a hand, which eventually she took, and he pulled the trembling girl to her feet. "He won't be bothering you again."

"Thank you," she gasped. Crying, Celine rubbed her eyes, wiped the tears from her face.

She did not notice him take out his knife, which he held behind his back now.

With his left hand he touched her cheek. "Forgive me."

She frowned, feeling apprehensive. "Forgive you, monsieur? Why should I need to forgive you when you just saved me?"

He smiled at her without baring his teeth. It was meant to be a reassuring smile. "No man will try to rape you again."

"Pardon?"

"It is for your own good," he muttered, suddenly pushing her against the wall and slashing at her with the knife she had not seen. Celine screamed, her arms coming up in front of her face in a defensive move, but it was no defence. Grabbing her wrists, he yanked her arms out of the way. Wielding his blade with a savage ferocity, the madman slashed again and again. Repeating over and over the words, "Forgive me; it is for your own good," as he cut her face.

He left her crying and bleeding on the cobbles.

Someone found her shortly after and she was taken to the nearest hospital.

'Lucky to be alive', they said. The girl would not have agreed with them.

The knifeman could have easily killed the young woman, yet instead he'd settled for destroying her good looks. However, this was no mercy for Mademoiselle Dupont. The poor girl wished she were dead when she finally saw the ruined visage that stared back at her from the mirror that had been kept from her for so long. She attempted to commit suicide, was unsuccessful and was eventually committed to an asylum.

The attack on Marie Monmarte was even more horrific.

It was the day her fiancé – Lieutenant Pierre Costain, an officer in the French cavalry – was due to arrive home in Paris on leave. Marie was eagerly awaiting his return and when there was a knock upon her door, instead of waiting for her maid to attend to it, she rushed to open it herself.

Her face was lit up with a radiant smile in anticipation of seeing her beloved and despite her disappointment at finding instead a stranger upon the doorstep, such was her good mood that the smile did not depart.

"Oh! I was expecting someone else."

"Forgive me, mademoiselle." Even though the stranger was dirty and dishevelled Marie's smile still remained in place.

"How can I help you?"

"I'm sorry; it is for your own good."

Before she could ask what was, the madman threw acid in her face. The attack left her screaming in agony, scarred and blinded. And Marie Monmarte never smiled again from that moment forward. She would have been unable to do so, even if she had ever felt any happiness in her life again.

Such was the damage caused to her countenance that some said it was a blessing that her eyes had been destroyed and she was unable to look upon her own reflection.

Marie never saw her fiancé again, nor, indeed, did he see her. When Lieutenant Costain should have been knocking upon Marie's door, he was, in fact, in the arms of another woman.

The lieutenant had already been contemplating ending their engagement, and when word reached him of the acid attack and the effect it had had upon his intended's beautiful features, he did so. Yet, not even once would Lieutenant Costain visit Marie, instead choosing to end their relationship by means of a letter, which, of course, had to be read to the poor girl.

Whether it was cowardice or callousness that played a part in his refusal to break the news to Marie in person is unknown. Certainly, Lieutenant Costain subsequently showed exceptional bravery in his military career when leading a cavalry charge against the Prussians. A charge that saw the French force suffer heavy casualties when it came under fire from the Prussian artillery's 6-pounder Krupp guns. The lieutenant was seriously wounded by the shrapnel from an exploding shell: his body and face being struck by zinc balls. Miraculously, he survived, but he was severely disfigured and blind in one eye.

Fortunately, for Paris's most noted beauties, the maniac who perpetrated these appalling acts was caught soon after the attack upon Mademoiselle Monmarte. Although it was when attempting another attack that he was apprehended, the target of his latest assault was not one of the city's many attractive women, nor even a native of Paris.

An artist, Luigi Strombolli was – as his name suggested – an Italian, originally from Naples.

The maniac's name was Jean Theroux. When he had learned that the celebrated painter was in Paris, Theroux knew he had to act.

Theroux had first encountered Strombolli some years before on Martinique. In those days, Theroux had been a sailor, ship's captain, no less, and the artist had been unknown outside of the Caribbean island that was part of the French colonial empire. Now, Theroux was living hand to mouth, barely keeping out of the gutter, whilst the artist was at the height of his popularity and was welcome at the most fashionable parties.

Renowned for his brilliant paintings, Strombolli was very skilled in another field, but society was unaware of this other artistic talent.

It was known, however, that Strombolli was in Paris seeking new models. And a new wife.

Only Theroux knew the ultimate fate that awaited those women. He believed he had good reason for carrying out these heinous attacks. He believed he was saving the women's lives by destroying their beauty.

As he spent the night brooding and drinking in the dosshouse, Jean Theroux had had a revelation and decided upon a new tactic. Rather than target any woman who might potentially capture the artist's interest, Theroux would strike directly at the man himself.

The party that was being held at the Rocheteau mansion in the *Faubourg Saint-Germain* district had been thrown in Strombolli's honour. Normally, in his current state Theroux would have been unable to gain admission. He had neglected his appearance for far too long, but in preparation for his reunion with the artist he had made good use of the public baths, not only to get clean, but also to steal some decent clothes.

It was a pleasant evening and many of the guests were outside on the terrace. Strombolli was at the heart of a clamouring throng. Beautiful women seeking the artist's attention. Unseen, Theroux approached from behind. He could have struck, the artist unaware of who his attacker was. But Theroux did not intend to kill. Theroux wanted him to suffer, as he had.

"Excuse me, Monsieur Strombolli."

"Yes?" Strombolli turned and frowned. There was something familiar about the man who had addressed him.

"It is true, is it not, that you are in Paris seeking a new wife?"

"It is true," Strombolli agreed. "And this city has so many delightful women to choose from." The artist smiled at those who surrounded him.

"It is quite a collection you are amassing. This will be the fifth, will it not?" It was Theroux who smiled now, and the lack of teeth in that smile, and the crooked nose, stirred distant memories for the artist.

There were a few gasps at both Theroux's toothless smile and his words, and someone whispered, 'bigamy'.

Strombolli ignored the question, focussing on Theorux's appearance instead. "My, my, it is a monster. Perhaps I should add you to my collection." The artist laughed, many of his female companions sharing his amusement.

"You are the monster!" Theroux cried in rage.

Laughter turned to screams of panic as Theroux lunged towards the artist's face with the knife he had suddenly pulled from inside his jacket.

Instinctively, Strombolli had thrown up his hands to protect

160

his handsome features. But Theroux had anticipated such a move, had hoped that that was how Strombolli would react, and changed his attack to slash at the artist's exposed hands.

Strombolli cried out as the knife struck, and Theroux launched himself at his enemy.

He had made sure the blade was extra sharp and by the time he was pulled from the artist, Strombolli's hands were a bloody ruin, missing several fingers.

Several years previously…

"Well, I can confirm your suspicions, dear lady." Doctor Badieur smiled at the young wife of Luigi Strombolli. "You are pregnant."

"Oh." Valerie Strombolli gasped at the news, her hand going to her open mouth.

And well she might gasp, the doctor thought. Before Luigi Strombolli had met his current wife, Doctor Badieur had performed tests that proved that the artist was unable to father children.

The young woman did her best to compose herself. "Please, Doctor Badieur, you will not tell my husband of my condition?" Madame Strombolli leaned forward in her chair. "I wish to break the … um … happy news to him myself."

Doctor Badieur wondered again whether she knew her husband was sterile. Should he warn her? Madame Strombolli was a beautiful woman, and obviously she was not averse to bestowing her favours upon other men. Perhaps she would be grateful for the warning. Perhaps she would want a secret abortion. He briefly imagined how she might show her gratitude. He quickly dismissed the idea and rose from his chair. Luigi Strombolli was not a man to fall foul of. If the artist suspected any liaison between his wife and his doctor then he would most certainly take action. No, it would not be wise to provoke the man. Badieur moved around the desk, took Madame Strombolli's hand and helped her rise. "Of course not." Although he would love to be there when she told her husband. "I am sure he will be most delighted."

It was three months later that the *Agnes Villiers* arrived in port. Upon his arrival, Jean Theroux booked into the most reputable inn then sent a message via the usual means – the teenage son of one of the native women who worked in the Strombolli kitchen – to let Valerie Strombolli know that he had returned to the island.

The ship's captain bathed and shaved, dressed in his best clothes, then settled down with a bottle of the finest available brandy to wait to hear from his lover. He waited several hours without receiving any response. Perhaps that was a response of sorts. He dismissed such thoughts from his head and ordered another bottle.

Eventually he decided it would be a good idea to go find Valerie Strombolli.

The Strombolli residence was a large whitewashed villa that stood at the heart of a sugar cane plantation. Strombolli's second wife had previously been married to the estate's owner Guy Le Roux. By all accounts, Le Roux was considered something of a bully and tyrant, and he had ruled the plantation with an iron fist.

One evening Le Roux was discovered hanging from a beam in an outhouse. No evidence of him suffering from depression was found and suicide was ruled out. With the death being deemed a murder, suspicion soon fell upon an ex-estate worker known only as Tomas.

Tomas had recently been dismissed by Le Roux after having a

heated argument with the plantation owner. Several witnesses testified he had sworn that he would have his revenge upon his former employer, and the fact that a small doll that bore a remarkable resemblance to Le Roux was discovered in his shack with a rope around its neck was enough for him to be declared guilty of the crime and subsequently executed by guillotine.

Luigi Strombolli had married the Widow Le Roux after a suitable period of mourning had passed.

Jean Theroux was somewhat inebriated by the time he reached the property. Ignoring discretion, he had gone straight to the front door and rapped upon it with the doorknocker, then after getting no response, banged with his fist. Still, no one came to the door. He knocked angrily upon it again, this time making his intentions clear vocally, "I wish to see Madame Strombolli!"

A native woman eventually opened the door. It was the kitchen servant, mother of the boy who carried Theroux's messages.

"Where's that lad of yours? Did he bring my message to your mistress? Or is he off spending my coin on the local whore?"

The woman scowled. "Go away!" she urged, gesturing that he should leave. "It is not possible."

"Where is she? I must see her."

"Go quickly, before the master comes." The servant tried to push him away. "You cannot see her."

From inside the house a man said, "Au contraire!" Luigi Strombolli was of above-average height, sturdy build, black-bearded and handsome. Nothing like the effeminate cuckold artist Theroux had imagined him to be. "You must see my wife, Captain Theroux. In fact, I insist upon it!" Strombolli smiled.

"Let him in, Marie. And then find Randolph and tell him to await me outside my private gallery."

The servant nodded, stood aside, to allow the captain to enter.

Theroux stepped inside. Marie closed the door and hastened

to carry out her instructions.

Strombolli looked the sailor up and down. "So you are the one." From his expression it was clear that he was not impressed by what he saw.

"You know?"

"Of course I know. Do you take me for a fool?"

"I love her."

"Yes, yes," Strombolli sighed. "Of course you do." He indicated that Theroux should follow him. "This way."

"I'll not give her up."

Strombolli led the way along a corridor the walls of which were lined with landscape paintings. If he'd had a mind to study them Theroux would have seen they were of a very good quality.

"Oh really? It may have escaped your notice, Captain Theroux, that she is *my* wife. *Mine!*"

"Damn you, Strombolli! You may be married to her, but it is me that she loves!"

"Once, she may have done. Not any longer."

"What do you mean?" Theroux snapped.

Strombolli ignored the question. "In here." He opened the door and entered the room.

Theroux followed, and Strombolli allowed the door to swing shut.

"Not many get to enter this room." The artist laughed. "Fewer get to leave it alive."

The walls of the room were also decorated with paintings. However, these were portraits rather than landscapes. All were of beautiful women. Often naked.

But Theroux's attention was captured by the tableau on the far side of the room.

A tableau composed of four women that were either standing or sitting quietly.

"Valerie!" Theroux had instantly recognised his lover.

She did not respond to his cry.

Theroux dashed across the room.

Strombolli followed at a more leisurely pace.

"My darling!"

To his horror, Captain Theroux realised that Valerie Strombolli did not move, nor did her three companions.

The sailor reached out to touch his love, but at the last moment he resisted the urge and span round to face the artist. "My God! What have you done?" He was shaking now. He felt sick.

"Quite a collection, isn't it? Allow me to introduce you to my first two wives: Sophia, and Claudette, and this is Alliette, a whore who once modelled for me." Strombolli smiled. It was a cruel, mocking smile. "Of course, you already know Valerie."

"What have you done?" Again, Theroux began to reach out to touch his lover, but he could not bring himself to make contact with the woman who stared glassily, whose smile was cold and fixed in place.

Instead, he lurched drunkenly at the artist.

Strombolli easily evaded the drunken sailor's attack. "Randolph!"

The ebony-coloured servant who entered at his master's call was a veritable giant. He rapidly crossed the room, and took hold of Captain Theroux. The sailor struggled to no avail. The servant had his burly arm around Theroux's throat and was crushing his windpipe.

"Now that you have seen my wife, perhaps you wish to die now. Well, do you wish to die, mon capitan?"

Theroux shook his head and managed to gasp, "No!"

Once he had stopped resisting, Randolph eased the pressure against his throat.

"In case you haven't already comprehended the situation I shall explain." The artist caressed Valerie Strombolli's cheek, ran the tip of his finger across her lips. "As well as being an extremely talented painter, I am also skilled at several other arts. One such that I am an expert in is taxidermy. As you can see." He indicated the four unmoving women. "Of course, it took a lot of practice to perfect the art, but I mastered the skills I needed before I began work on Sophia, my first wife."

"You monster!"

"Valerie brought this upon herself with her infidelity. Or rather brought it about sooner. This would have always been her fate. Before her beauty started to fade. When that happens, well an artist needs a new muse, new inspiration. A new model. A new wife."

Theroux started to struggle again. "I'll kill you!"

"I think not." Strombolli nodded to his servant, who increased the pressure against Theroux's throat. "Randolph, take him outside."

Once out in the courtyard to the rear of the house the servant threw Theroux to the ground. A grim-faced plantation labourer leaned against a wall. He sprang to attention once he saw his master emerge from the house.

"Ah, Doctor Lorencio. We will have need of your services soon. You are prepared?"

The labourer held up a canvas bag and nodded.

"Good."

Randolph removed his jacket and handed it to the kitchen servant who took it inside.

"Beat him," commanded Strombolli, who then addressed Theroux, "Much as I would enjoy administering this beating myself I cannot risk damaging my hands. You do understand, I'm sure. No matter, this is something that Randolph has a talent for and he will do a more than adequate job."

Randolph rolled up the sleeves of his shirt as he strode over to where Captain Theroux sprawled face down in the dirt, gasping for breath. He spat at the downed man then proceeded to kick him. After striking the writhing sailor several times with his booted foot the servant grabbed Theroux by the hair, pulled him up and punched him repeatedly.

"Pay especial consideration to the captain's face, Randolph. I cannot see any appeal in it myself, yet evidently some women find it attractive. We do not want that to occur ever again."

Randolph was merciless. In fact, he took great pleasure in his brutality. Eventually he dragged the almost-comatose sailor across the courtyard and slammed his face against the wall.

The sailor's nose was broken and several teeth now lay in the bloodied courtyard dirt.

Strombolli watched impassively until he was satisfied. "Enough, Randolph. I think that is sufficient."

Randolph grinned and released his hold on the battered and bruised ship's captain, allowing him to fall to the ground.

"Doctor Lorencio!" Strombolli called. "I think it is time for you to attend to your patient."

The labourer came running. He knelt beside the sailor, reached into his bag of tools, and took out the instrument he needed to use on Theroux. He adjusted the sailor's clothing so he could perform the prescribed surgery.

The surgery prescribed by his master.

Doctor Lorencio licked his lips, muttered a prayer, and set to work.

And Jean Theroux shrieked in agony as Doctor Lorencio operated upon him with a *castratori*.

Once severed, the labourer held up Theroux's testicles for Strombolli's approval.

"Very good." Luigi Strombolli clapped his hands. "Now there'll be no more seducing other men's wives for you, captain." He turned to go back into the villa, but then paused as if remembering something.

"Oh, there's one more thing ... Marie!" Strombolli gave a nod of his head and the kitchen servant who had been waiting for the signal emerged from the house. She was carrying a wooden box, which she placed on the ground in front of the wailing Theroux and beside his testicles, which Lorencio had quickly dropped.

"I think that this belongs to you." Strombolli's lip curled into a sneer. Laughing, he went inside.

Randolph crouched next to the sailor and shook him. "Open it, damn you!"

Slowly, Theroux reached out and removed the lid. Inside the box was a sealed glass jar.

Randolph grinned. "Only the master gets to stuff his wife."

The jar contained a solution of formaldehyde that preserved a human foetus.

www.ingramcontent.com/pod-product-compliance
Lightning Source LLC
Chambersburg PA
CBHW070036260626
47159CB00005B/2059